BAD FEELING

S. Markham

MINERVA PRESS

LONDON
MONTREUX LOS ANGELES SYDNEY

BAD FEELING
Copyright © S. Markham 1998

All Rights Reserved

ISBN 1 86106 788 7

First Published 1998 by
MINERVA PRESS
195 Knightsbridge
London SW7 1RE

Printed in Great Britain for Minerva Press

BAD FEELING

Contents

Chapter One

Contact

Sunshine in January, how glorious! Kim had to suppress a wild desire to skip as she sped along the pavement, clutching a borrowed copy of *The Catcher in the Rye*. Glancing up at an approaching cyclist, she was surprised to find that she recognised him. It was Jamie Albury, a guy she had known at sixth-form college. She smiled at him. He cycled over to her and dismounted.

"Hi Kim! It's good to see you, it must be four years..."

"Yeah, ancient history. How are you?"

"Fine, and you?"

"Much better than I have been recently," she replied with a mock grimace.

"Yeah, you're almost..."

He stopped and Kim grinned at him. "What?"

"I saw you some time ago and I wasn't sure if it was you or not, you looked so old. I thought it was your mum or something."

"Thanks. Yes, I was rather emaciated wasn't I?" Kim took a deep breath, "So what have you been up to?" she asked.

"I'm in a band with some of my mates, we play cover versions and some of our own stuff locally."

"That's great! I've got a friend, Chris, who's studying English at York – he lent me this copy of *Catcher* – anyway, he's doing something similar with three of his mates. They call themselves the 'Laughing Maggots', it's quite appropriate really!"

"Never heard of them."

"I'm not surprised. I doubt if you've missed anything though... Well good luck, I'll keep an eye out for you appearing on the covers of music magazines."

"More like *Crime Weekly*."

Kim laughed, her copper-coloured hair waving exuberantly about her face.

"Oh, by the way, I call myself Jay rather than Jamie nowadays."

"I see, cool."

"Yeah, so what are you doing? It must be almost a year since you graduated."

"Deciding what to do next. I needed some time to sort myself out after my flirtation with death. I guess that this is the calm before the storm."

"I can understand that."

"Bye Jay."

"Bye, take care."

She turned, then waved at him as she walked away. He had remembered her. When Kim first met Jay, at sixth-form college, he had struck her as being one of the 'in' guys and therefore too cool to be interested in her. She had been surprised and more than a little suspicious when he had started to talk to her, a redhead with a high IQ. She had thought that he was trying to take the piss. She was wrong, he had liked her because she was different from the other girls; very intelligent, with a cool wit and latent wild streak.

They had talked philosophy, guitars and Steve Vai. Very sixth-form, but fun.

After doing her A levels, she had gone up to Cambridge and lost track of him. She'd heard that he hadn't done very well, but nothing more. Still, it had been good to see him again.

Chapter Two

And After

Winter

Kim, clad in a short black dress, sheer black tights, brilliant white ankle socks and small black boots, was sitting in the kitchen of the small rented house which Jay shared with his elder sister, staring out of the window into the back garden. He had called out to her as she passed by and had asked her if she wanted to come in out of the cold and have a drink. She had accepted without reservation.

"Coffee, Kim?"

"Fine, black no sugar."

Jay poured boiling water into a pale green mug and handed it to her.

"So what are you doing now?"

"I'm thinking of going into teaching."

"Good luck, you'll need it," he said, noticing a dark blue stain on the middle finger of her left hand. "Have you been writing?"

"Yep. I'm trying to write a novel... note the emphasis on 'trying'."

She smiled sheepishly.

"The phantom scribbler strikes again! What's it about?"

Kim shifted uneasily on her stool. "I'd rather not say, it would only sound silly. I suppose you could call it a witness to personal heroism, although it's mainly about self-deception. Anyway, it isn't so much the plot as what hangs on it which makes it the creature it is."

"Intriguing. You're not writing erotica are you?"

"Hardly!" she squeaked, "That would be too tacky. Besides, it has all been done before." Why, is that how you see me, as an erotomaniac?"

"You never can tell with some people."

Kim shot him a fierce look, then pointed to a packet on the shelf beside her. "Protein powder, what's that for?"

"Body-building."

"You don't do that, do you? There's nothing worse than men who have so much designer muscle that they look like pieces of leather upholstery."

Jay shrugged and put his coffee mug into the sink. Looking up at her again he asked, "Did you really fancy that physics teacher?"

"No way. The thing was that he used to stereotype me as some kind of megaswot. It really used to annoy me. He once said to me, 'You know, Kim, you really ought to read about things other than physics.' How dare he make the assumption that he knew what I did and didn't read? What was worse, I didn't even read physics and he made me feel guilty for not doing so, as if I had failed his expectations of me. I hated it, so I decided to twist the stereotype by faking a crush on him. He actually believed it! Honestly, the arrogance of thirty-something males. Huh!"

Jay laughed. "Would you have had an affair with him if you'd had the opportunity?"

"Maybe... out of curiosity. No, the teacher I did fancy was the guy who taught me chemistry."

"He never taught me."

"No? Oh, but I was so in lust with him. He had this unbelievable body, I think he used to play a lot of squash or something. He didn't like me much, he used to get really mad at me because he thought I was an intellectual snob. 'Practical chemistry is important as well as theory, Kim,' he'd say, his eyes positively darting about from side to side in anger. I used to love it."

Kim closed her eyes as if trying to recapture the moment.

Jay broke her reverie.

"You liked annoying people didn't you?"

"Only when I found it sexually stimulating."

"I think it's because you're intrinsically provocative."

"Who knows?"

"Are you going out with anyone at the moment?"

"No way. Whenever I'm with a guy, I always end up feeling as if I'm performing for him. I can never seem to be myself."

"That would be too frightening."

"Ha, ha, ha," drawled Kim, grinning at Jay. "Are you still with Mandy?"

"Yeah," his voice lacked enthusiasm.

"Long time."

"Seems like forever, but I've never mentioned the L-word to her."

"What's that?"

"Love."

"Oh, I see..." Kim bit her lip. "Why do you find it so hard to say?"

She stared at him, her eyes opening wide, "What are you afraid of?"

"Being tied down. When you're in a relationship you have to think for two people. Sometimes she wants to be with me and I just want to be on my own or with my mates, watching the footy, etc. That really pisses me off."

"I know what you mean... I haven't had a boyfriend since I nearly starved myself to death..." Kim frowned and stared down at her socks.

"Do you mind?"

"No! Not every girl needs a man to feel complete, you know. I don't need some male to maintain my self-esteem, and my sense of my own identity is too strong and sure to be forfeited for any man."

"Okay, no need to get excited, I wish I hadn't said anything now."

"I'm sorry... but sex is ridiculous, it's just so incongruous, and who in their right mind wants to fuck up their biochemistry with little white pills anyway? I prefer to sleep alone, just me and my teddy bear." Kim paused and relaxed. "It beats me how any woman could ever want to sleep with another man once she's seen how they look in the morning. I have, and it isn't pretty."

"Likewise," said Jay, scratching his arm.

Kim watched him. "At least women aren't as hairy as men," she retorted.

"Wanna bet? You haven't seen what I've seen."

"I wouldn't want to!" she said, laughing.

Jay stared at her hollow cheeks. "So why did you stop eating? If you don't mind me asking."

Kim's smile froze. "That's one of the not-so-great unsolved mysteries of my life," she said slowly. "I didn't stop eating, I was just gradually eating less and less, that's all." She folded her arms across her chest.

"That's all? It sounds like a pretty big deal to me."

"Yes, I guess it was, very dangerous and very unnecessary," she shrugged.

"So why did you do it, did some guy fuck you up?"

"You're so eloquent, Jay." Her voice was hollow.

"Yeah, well, you might have died."

Kim's eyes met his. "Or if not that, gone blind or something, I know... but no, no guy has ever 'fucked me up' in any way whatsoever, no mere man could make me do that to myself, there are some things that only you can do to yourself. I think it was that the hunger made me feel alive, almost high... more blood to the brain if the stomach doesn't need it, I guess. I liked the feeling of martyrdom it inspired. And I think that part of me resented being dependent on a collection of chaotically coordinated chemical couplings to sustain my life."

"That sounds like you."

"Mmm... Let's change the subject. You don't want to ever get married then?"

"Not likely." A flicker of panic passed across Jay's face. "I couldn't stand the responsibility of having to look after someone else, I can't even look after myself."

"I know what you mean, I think marriage would be the kiss of death."

"Yeah, for the poor guy who married you."

"Very funny," she said dryly, "but marriage is a slow form of suicide.

Mundanity quenches passion. Married couples are so boring, so many commitments. I couldn't bear it, it must really age you. I intend to be twenty-two going on nineteen for life. And I don't want a partner either, I couldn't bear to live with someone on a permanent basis."

"I thought men were supposed to be the only ones who were afraid to commit."

"Don't be sexist."

"Kids are even worse."

"I know, I can't stand babies or anything amorphous in mind or body."

"Yeah, they're just like maggots, but with fat little arms and legs."

"You bet. Pregnancy is just one big hormonefest. I'll never understand how some women can willingly subject themselves to those anabolic processes. They must be suffering some form of psychosis. I reckon it's only when women become bored with their lives on some level that basic instinct takes over and they begin to want to have babies."

"It makes me glad to be male."

"Yeah, it's madness. I have a friend, Laura, who I met at university. She's a bisexual, feminist medic and even she wants to have two kids; no husband mind, just the children. She says your body compensates, but somehow I don't think so." Kim smiled wryly to herself. Why was Jay so eager to accept her over-simplistic views? Was it insecurity or downright fear?

"Do you remember Ian Gibson?" he asked.

"Yes."

"He used to be in the band before he met this girl and lost interest.

Now he's married and has two kids. He always said as he'd never have a family after seeing what his parents went through when they split up. It's unbelievable."

"Poor guy, two kids... yeuch!"

"You really hate kids, don't you?"

"I wouldn't go that far, they're okay if kept at a distance, the farther the better. No, I just have a natural antipathy for anything amorphous in mind and body, and kids are it."

"I don't suppose you've ever been in love?"

"No, never. I have a bloodless heart. And you?"

"No."

Kim smiled, "Oh come on, Jay, don't be coy. I know men are supposed to find it hard to talk about their feelings, but you shouldn't have any inhibitions when you're with me. I won't tell anyone what you say. I'm not like other girls, I'm neutral."

"No, I've never been in love."

"I don't think I could love anyone. Human beings are, without exception, fatally flawed. I might love being with someone, or the things which make them who they are, but nothing more, not them. I suppose I'm a cold bitch, but I don't want to be bound to someone by emotional ties. Bonding never exists without bondage."

"The trouble with most women is that they want to mould their men into what they think they should be."

"I'd never do that, I know how much I'd resent it if anyone tried to change me. That's the trouble with 'explicit' love, it's possessive and manipulative. I prefer feelings to be implicit; subtle, not binding. I want to be free to be blown on the wind of desire. I don't want a boyfriend, I want a partner in crime."

"That's what I like about you, you're so radical."

Kim laughed. "I'm not sure if that's such a good thing. I'm very bad at communicating how I feel to others, being terribly uncomfortable with sentences involving more that one pronoun, especially if they're 'you' and 'me'. My mien is rarely in phase with my mind."

"Have you ever been badly hurt by someone?"

"No, I've never had that luxury."

"You don't know how lucky you are. There are basically two types of men in the world; those who try to frighten their women into bed with them, and studenty types, like me, who pretend to be interested in the girl for her mind. But at the end of the day both types only want to get their leg over."

"You're so cynical, Jay."

"I've sometimes wondered what it would be like to have sex with you."

"You wouldn't enjoy it, I tend to trip out on my own. Not everyone is up to the ride."

Jay grinned. "Do you make a lot of noise?" He wouldn't mind hearing her scream for him.

"I'm usually too far gone to notice."

"I remember thinking, when I knew you in the sixth form, that you had eliminated the need for sex from your life."

"Oh you did, did you?" Kim sounded slightly bemused. "I think that at that time in my life the only guys I fancied were either dead, homosexual or fictional. I was aware of my sexuality, but I didn't want it to hijack my life."

Early Spring

Kim spun round, shaken from her reverie by the touch of a hand on her shoulder. She had been swimming and was walking home. Turning round, she found Jay behind her, his long hair dyed blonde.

"Hi Kim, aren't you cold without a coat?"

"A little, but I like to feel the cold etch into me, it makes me feel alive."

"Rather you than me."

"Maybe my blood runs faster than yours."

"You were walking fast, were you going anywhere special?"

"Only in my mind," she laughed.

"Look, I don't want this to be a regular thing, but would you like to go for a walk?"

"Sure," Kim replied, giving Jay a strange look; was he insecure or just plain arrogant?"

"It's just that I'm a great believer in familiarity breeding contempt."

"That's okay, I understand... I see you've dyed your hair."

"Yeah, the first time I did it, it turned out all gingery and I wasn't having that... no disrespect to you..."

Kim fingered her long, red locks self-consciously.

"...but it's okay now."

"Yes, it looks good, you look more like Brad Pitt every time I see you."

"Thanks, I'll take that as a compliment. Oh, by the way, I've split up with Mandy," he continued in less happy tones.

Kim made a slight frown, "Oh, I'm sorry, Jay."

"Yeah, I felt that I didn't have enough freedom. Besides, it had got to the point that when the mood struck I had more inclination to reach for myself than for her."

"So how do you feel now?"

"Pretty bad, I can't stop thinking about her. I'm really depressed."

"That's tough. Have you tried writing your feelings down, that can help? Use it as a source of inspiration for a song."

"Nah, it would only be sentimental shite. I can't get her out of my mind. I don't know what to do. I saw her yesterday in town and we spoke to each other. Part of me wanted to get back with her and part of me didn't."

Kim made what she hoped were sympathetic noises. It

was sad that he was so strung out on Mandy.

"I'm glad that I can talk to you about this, Kim. It's easier to talk to women than to men, they're less competitive and more understanding."

"I wish I could say something that would help."

"It's just that I can't think of anything else, it's really getting me down. I'm turning into a complete crisp junkie... and I really miss the sex."

"You can always wank off," Kim said. A little levity never hurt anyone.

"I do that anyway."

"You've still got the band."

"Yeah, that's another thing, Nick has been turning up late for practices. We've had to question him about his commitment."

"How did it go?"

"Okay. We were on space hoppers at the time."

"What?" Kim almost choked, "You mean the drugs or the orange, bouncy things?"

"What do you think?"

Two blondes cycled past. Kim stared wistfully after them. Jay watched her.

"Too fat," he said.

"Too blonde," replied Kim, "one's enough, two's just too much!"

Jay laughed. Kim's mind flicked to the posters she'd seen pinned on Jay's wall. "How can you drool over all those blonde bimbos? They're so tacky. Doesn't it strike you as pathetic that men degrade themselves in that way?"

"It's the nature of the beast, I guess."

"I give up, you're too far gone... the cult of the blonde. It's all social conditioning, you know. I remember that when I was six I was given a Sindy doll, my one and only

Sindy I hasten to add, I was always more of a teddy bear girl... anyway, I was dead disappointed that I'd been given a blonde instead of a brunette. Somehow, between then and now I've been brainwashed into thinking that blonde is best."

"They don't make redhead Sindys, do they?"

"Very funny, there's nothing wrong with being a coppertop."

"Done much scribbling recently?"

"Don't mention that, please."

"Not too good then?"

"No, quite the reverse, the more I write, the more I want to write, I think I may have become addicted. I must be on a roll; I sit down, I switch the radio on, pick up my pen and I'm away."

"You're not on anything, are you?"

"Not unless you count caffeine. I haven't read anything for weeks, it just seems so passive to read someone else's words rather than write my own. I've just been swimming to escape."

"The loneliness of the longhand writer."

"Yeah, something like that."

A stray dog came up to them and nuzzled Kim. She flinched and brushed it away. Jay bent down and stroked it. Looking up at Kim he asked, "Don't you like dogs?"

"Not when they have teeth I don't."

"I got a golden retriever pup when I was two. We grew up together, it really cut me up when he died."

"That's so sad."

"Well, since you clearly think I'm obsessed with blondes, you might as well tell me about your dark dreams and fantasies."

"I don't really have any... although sometimes, when I'm wet and cold and far from home, I imagine I'm in a room with all the men I've ever hated and they're all tied up with nowhere to go. I'm sitting there, amongst them, listening to my favourite tapes and polishing a gun. They know that sooner or later I'm going to shoot one of them, but they don't know who or when."

"Cool."

Summer

Kim had gone round to Jay's house on the off chance of finding him in.

She was in luck.

"Do you want to sit outside in the garden, Kim?"

"Okay."

The sun was dazzling. Jay raised a hand to his eyes to shield them from the burning rays. "I could stay out here forever," he murmured.

"Mmm, summertime, when the freckles come out in full force."

Jay turned and stared hard at Kim's face. "Oh yeah," he drawled, "so they have."

Kim cringed, "I wish I'd kept my mouth shut now."

"I like them, I think they make you look spunky. Aren't you going to take your shirt off? It's so hot out here, I could rip my skin off."

"Okay, I don't think that I've anything incriminating written on my arms." She peeled off her pale pink shirt to reveal sunkissed arms, her torso clad in a thin white T-shirt.

"What?"

"Just notes. If I get a 'literary inspiration' – ha ha – and there is no paper around, I use my skin."

"And I suppose that if you haven't got a pen you open up a vein and draw blood."

"I don't go quite that far."

"Yeah, I remember when I once went round to your house just before the A levels, you had stuff written on your right arm then."

"Yes, chemistry revision notes. They were scrubbed off long before I sat the exam, of course."

"Of course."

"It's nothing compared to what I did for my biology O level," she laughed, "I actually went as far as labelling the various parts of my body with the name of the corresponding bone in an attempt to learn them. Dedication or what?"

"I suppose the end justified the means."

"Yeah."

"Hey, I'm going to get myself a Coke, would you like one?"

"No thanks, I'm fine."

Jay disappeared into the house. Kim lay back on the grass and closed her eyes, revelling in the delicious feel of the sun's warmth on her bare skin. Jay returned and sat down beside her, "Oh, by the way, I'm back with Mandy again."

"Good."

"We've got more freedom in our relationship now, it's better for me and I think it's better for her."

"Mmm... did I ever tell you about the time Michael Bradley tried to seduce me?"

"You're kidding?"

"'Fraid not. It happened in the summer holidays after the A levels. He asked me to come round to his house to talk about some programme he'd seen on TV."

"Sure." Jay's voice had a sarcastic edge.

"That's what I thought, but I decided to go round just to satisfy my curiosity."

"What happened?"

"Not a lot. He did Freudian regression on me in his room, you know 'What's your earliest memory?' etc., I think he got it from his social biology A level. Then he made me lie on the bed whilst he touched my body in various places and measured my pulse."

"And you let him do that?" Jay squeaked.

"Well, it was him making a fool of himself, not me." Kim's voice was thick with distaste, "Yeuch, it makes my skin crawl just thinking about it."

"What a wanker."

"I know. After that he said he was just going out of his room for a minute and disappeared. When he came back he was only wearing boxer shorts. He said that he wasn't going to make me do anything I didn't want to – he got that right – but if I wanted to we could give each other pleasure. It was awful."

"So what did you do?"

"I said no, of course, and made a quick exit."

"What a dickhead... what would you do if I tried anything like that?"

"You wouldn't see me for dust."

"That's what I thought. So you don't fancy me then?"

Kim cleared her throat, "I never answer questions like that."

"Okay, you're an honest girl, I'll take that as a no."

"I didn't say that, I simply don't like power games."
Kim frowned.

"To change the subject, I hope you don't mind me
asking, but what does your dad do?"

"Strange question... um, he's a solicitor, always under
stress."

"Oh, very professional. So what happened with you,
Jay?"

"I was a lazy bastard, I just didn't work hard enough," he
grinned.

"My parents are a couple of duds." She took a deep
breath, "I don't think my mother's ever said anything
remotely intelligent or original in her life and as for Dad,
he's a total gutless wonder. Throughout his life he has
simply let things happen to him. He seems to exist in a
state of permanent perplexity, I've even heard him
whimpering to himself when he's doing something he
doesn't like."

"You're really hung up on this, aren't you?" Jay said in a
quiet voice.

"No, not really. I'm sorry for going on like that. I guess
I have some resentments which I find it hard to forget."

"Don't we all. You're okay. You must be the second
most intelligent person I know."

"Not the first?" she cried in mock horror.

"No, that accolade goes to one of my other mates, into
mysticism and stuff. He wears pretty bizarre stuff, but he
won't take any shit from anyone. It was through him that I
got into philosophy and stuff; Nietzsche, Wittgenstein, etc.
But the last time I saw him he was going on about how
values in society are declining and I was out of there like a
shot."

"Why? Does morality scare you?"

"No, I *used* to try and act morally, but it didn't work out, I'm more of an amoral person."

Surprise, surprise. A moral Jay? No, it was impossible to imagine such a creature. Jay was a bad boy and good at it.

"I think morality rests on not hurting people unless it's absolutely unavoidable," said Kim flatly.

"So people will like you and think you a good person." Jay spoke with thinly veiled sarcasm. Kim gave him a startled look.

"I only hate in self-defence," she said levelly, "if someone is unpleasant it's a sure sign they're not comfortable in their own skin."

"Yeah, I suppose there's something in that," Jay agreed, relaxing.

"You're okay Kim, I think you're the coolest uncool person I know." Damn her with faint praise.

"Thanks... I think. Isn't that like saying I'm the tallest midget you know, or something?" She smiled and looked at her watch. "Oh well, I must disappear now, nice to talk to you, Jay."

"Likewise," he smiled back at her.

As he walked with her to the front door he said, "Tell me, Kim, what do you dream about?"

"Hmm, everything and nothing. Actually, I dreamt about you last night."

"Go on."

"I was walking in the grounds of an ancient castle and I saw you sitting on the grass with a group of girls. I went up to them and said 'Hi'. Then I bent down and kissed you on the lips," Kim stared down at her T-shirt, then raised her eyes to his face. "I was afraid that you would glare at me or

worse, but when I looked into your eyes I saw nothing."
She frowned.

"Well, that's a start," said Jay staring fixedly at her, his
face distorted by an animal grin.

Kim sensed her identity shift and change within her as a
wave of nausea washed through her, leaving her feeling
weak. She swallowed.

"Bye Jay."

Chapter Three

One Day

Kim felt herself light up inside when she saw Jay cycling towards her. He was wearing shorts and a pale blue denim jacket, and he was smiling.

"Hi," he said as he got off his cycle.

"Hi, have you been on holiday yet?"

"I would be browner than this if I had. I'm going to Cyprus with Mandy in a couple of weeks."

"Good, I hope you enjoy it. I'm going to stay with one of my old university friends in Derbyshire for a few days... So, how is Mandy?"

"Okay, she's starting an art course in Sheffield in September."

"Good for her. What does she want to do afterwards?"

"She doesn't know, she isn't a very decisive person."

Looking at Kim, Jay noticed that she had lost weight. "You look thinner than usual, you haven't started on the starvation thing again, have you?"

Kim frowned. "I don't know, maybe. I've been spending a lot of time writing. I like being able to bend words to my will; it gives me such a buzz that I tend to forget to eat until I get the aches or the shakes."

Jay stared hard at Kim and she looked away from him, running a tanned hand through her amber hair.

"You're not going to hurt yourself again, are you?"

"I didn't try to in the first place, it just happened," she replied in a tight voice.

Jay decided to drop the subject. "Like to go for a walk?"

"Sure," Kim smiled. The tension evaporated.

"Where do you want to go?"

"Over the fields and far away," she said wistfully.

After Jay had dropped his cycle and jacket off at his home they walked into some playing fields and headed for the stretches of arable land beyond. Jay jumped easily over the wire boundary fence, but Kim, awkward whenever anything even remotely gymnastic was required of her, managed to get her pump stuck and fell onto her right leg.

"Are you all right?"

Kim, shaking with laughter, replied in the affirmative, "I'll be okay in a minute." She rubbed her injured limb.

"I thought you were fit," said Jay, staring down at her. Her body certainly gave the impression of fitness; from the look of those legs she had dancers' muscles.

"I am," she protested, "it was that wretched fence, it has it in for me."

"Is that blood on your sock?"

"Umm yeah, but it's an old stain. Sometimes my toes bleed if I walk too far in hot weather."

"You're sure it isn't any other kind of blood?"

"What?" Kim looked up at Jay. He was smirking. "Oh... you mean blood, but not as guys know it. No it isn't, I haven't bled in that way for three years. I must have a low hormone count or something."

"Why? Because you starved yourself?"

Kim wished he wouldn't keep mentioning that.

"No, it stopped long before that sorry little episode. A case of mind over matter, I think. I don't need that kind of blood."

Kim, the goddess of purity and sterility.

She got to her feet and they walked on, Kim behind Jay along the narrow footpaths which bordered the strips of barley. Kim seized an ear of the grain, shredded it in the palm of her left hand and tossed a few grains onto Jay's bare back.

"You've got spots," she teased.

"Have I?" He sounded annoyed, "Well I'm sure your body isn't perfect either."

"Oh, my body's far from perfect," she replied slowly, "especially my leg!"

Jay laughed. "No, I'm just a skinny bastard. I often get marks on my back from weightlifting. They make Mandy dead suspicious, she thinks that I'm having it off with someone else."

"Poor you," Kim said in a slightly mocking tone of voice.

"You're okay. You've got a nice voice. It's only when people look at you that they go yuuuk."

"Thanks," she said drily.

"Naaa..." he drawled and turning round, briefly put his arm around her shoulder. Kim shook herself free.

"I knew a guy at Cambridge, called Simon; he had a beautiful voice, one without so much as a hint of arrogance or accent."

"I know what you mean. I've a mate with a great voice; he can make the lasses do anything for him. All he has to do is say 'Will you make me a cup of tea'," Jay mimicked in a husky voice, "and they do it. I can't make them do shit for me."

"Awww."

"Yeah, it's a hard life."

Kim paused. "How many people have you slept with?"

It must have been the sun that made her ask.

"Five or six."

"Only five or six?" She sounded almost disappointed.

"Don't sound so incredulous. I didn't sleep with anyone until I was twenty, I didn't think that any girl deserved to see my dick."

Kim almost choked, "No, I can't imagine what any girl could have done to deserve that."

"Very funny, now it's your turn."

"Pardon?"

"I reckon that you were a virgin before you went to university, right?"

"Maybe."

"And I think that you've slept with two men since."

"Two? Why two?"

"Am I right?"

"Ha... I'm not saying."

"Why not?"

"I just don't want to. Okay?"

"Okay, if you don't want to, I can't make you."

Too right he couldn't.

"I don't like to tell guys that sort of thing about myself."

"So you talk about it to women?"

"That's different."

"Why?"

"Because guys make it so, that's why."

They fell silent. Kim was thinking about Simon, the first man she had slept with. Her heart still ached for him and she hated herself for it. Suddenly Jay stopped walking, turned round, and looked Kim straight in the eye.

"Okay, but you're going to have to pay a forfeit."

"Oh really, what?" She sounded nonchalant.

"You have to tell me what you hate most about yourself."

Was that all? "Okay, umm... right, I have a bad tendency to disassociate myself from my past."

"Sounds psycho."

"Not really, it's just that I'm a solipsist at heart."

"I rest my case."

Kim smiled, "Well you did ask, and you know what they say about asking stupid questions."

"Yeah, okay. So what kind of sex do you like? Or do you disassociate yourself from that too?"

"Aggressive sex, with teeth and claws. I'm a closet vampire at heart, so there must be blood."

Kim: true daughter of decadence.

"If you bit me you'd get a slap."

"In your dreams, boy."

Kim grinned to herself, now there was an idea.

"So violence turns you on?"

"No, it's the truth that turns me on; there's more than one way to be naked with another human being."

"You'll probably hit me if I ask you this..." Jay began, the blood hot in his face.

"No I won't. You can ask me anything you like, it's only words after all."

This sounded interesting.

"Okay, it's just that you don't strike me as a girl who masturbates a lot."

Yuk! Kim hated that word.

"I never do it. I prefer the real thing." Well she wasn't going to tell him the truth, was she? "Hey Jay, I don't do it because I'm so sensitive down there that one touch makes me shoot off the bed."

Jay flicked his tongue over his lips. "It's a good way of getting to know what you like."

"Maybe."

They walked into a small copse. Shafts of light fell through the trees and onto the path they were following. A profusion of orange-and-black-winged tortoiseshell butterflies danced before their eyes.

"Okay Jay, when was the last time you had sex... with someone else in the same room?"

"Ha, fucking ha. Last night, just after midnight."

"Mmm, what was I doing then?" mused Kim.

"Probably asleep."

"No, I wasn't actually. I was reading *The Fall of Hyperion*."

"The fall of what?" Jay laughed.

"Hyperion," she replied, letting each syllable roll majestically off her tongue, "and I bet I had a better time than you."

"You probably did, it wasn't too good last night, I was too tired."

They had come full circle and were approaching the edge of the fields. Turning to Kim, Jay said, "I'm going to ask you something, but don't say yes or no."

"Okay," said Kim mystified.

"I'll be in at eight tonight and if you come round we can have sex. My sister won't be there, she's on the night shift."

"This isn't a joke, is it?"

"No. I wanted to take you when we were in the fields, but I didn't have anything with me."

"Okay."

★

Jay was watching football in the kitchen when Kim arrived wearing a long, black summer dress and a purple ribbon in her hair.

"Do you mind if I finish watching this? I know it's a bit functional in here, but..."

"That's okay, I don't mind."

Kim flicked through a tabloid newspaper whilst she waited. Then they went into the sitting room. It was decorated with birthday cards.

"Do you want a drink?"

"Water would be fine."

"I mean a proper drink."

"Okay. Orange juice? I don't do ethanol, I don't like the taste."

"Coming up."

Jay disappeared, then returned with her juice and a Coke for himself. They talked for a while about pseudo-philosophies and the paranormal. Jay was seriously interested in the latter, Kim was more sceptical, playing Scully to his Mulder.

"I think that black magic appeals most to those people who have least control over their lives. They lack the intelligence and willpower to affect changes in the real world, so they bury themselves in a miasma of lies and rituals..."

"But isn't Christianity like that?" interrupted Jay.

"All belief systems are like that, even mathematics and science to a certain extent, with their unproven axioms and laws."

"So you don't believe in black magic then?"

"I think it may 'work' in certain circumstances, but not in the way people imagine it might. I think that all the rituals and associated paraphernalia can help you to focus your thoughts on something and thus clarify your desires and intentions, so that you're more aware of what you want to achieve. You're more likely to get what you want if you set about pursuing it with a clear mind."

Jay watched Kim as she spoke, her head turned slightly away from him. He studied her profile and form. She was beautiful; small and dainty, her hair dark red in the shadows of the sitting room. There was something almost exotic about her. She was gorgeous, far better looking than Mandy; mocha to his girlfriend's vanilla... and she had a brain... and she was here with him.

She stopped speaking.

"Did you ever have a near-death experience when you got so thin?" he asked.

Kim turned and looked him straight in the eye, noticing how strange his pupils appeared: encircled with light reflected from she knew not where.

"No, but I probably got as close to one as is humanly possible without it happening," she replied levelly.

"I've a mate who claims that he's experienced astral projection. Apparently, it only happens if you're prepared to give up your sense of self-importance... and sex. I could never do that."

"Surprise, surprise," mocked Kim.

The doorbell rang.

"Shushhh," hissed Jay.

They waited. Silence.

"Okay, carry on," he said, "but whisper."

"I think you were talking about astral projection," she replied in low, precise tones.

"Oh yeah, anyway I've been reading about dreams too. There are these mental exercises you can do if you want to gain control of your own dreams. I've tried them all, but they don't seem to work for me."

"Perhaps you're trying too hard, or approaching it in the wrong manner."

"What do you mean?"

"You have to let them affect you viscerally as well as cerebrally if you want to influence your subconscious."

Jay was silent, lost in thought. Kim, bored, fiddled with her hair.

Eventually she said, "Have you ever done drugs, Jay?"

"No," he replied in a hard voice.

"Have you ever been offered any?"

"All the time, I was offered some this morning."

"So why haven't you tried any?"

Jay shot her a penetrating look. "Because they're addictive."

He sounded uncharacteristically serious. There was something wrong here, but she couldn't quite put her finger on it. She decided to change the subject.

"Don't you care about being unfaithful to your girlfriend?"

"That's a killer... eh, no, I don't."

"Why not? It would hurt her an awful lot if she found out."

"It's got nothing to do with her. Besides, what she doesn't know can't hurt her."

"Fidelity equals possession?"

"If you like... Will you please stop clawing that sofa arm? You're going to rip it to shreds with those talons of yours if you're not careful."

"Sorry." Kim relaxed her grip on the upholstery; she hadn't realised how deeply she had dug her nails into it.

"Does it bother you?" he asked.

"No," she said quietly, "not in the least. I think one should be free to be as intimate as one chooses with other people, provided there's mutual consent."

Kim knew where Jay was coming from – pure self. Still, at least he was honest about it. Most people weren't, not even to themselves. She couldn't stand hypocrites.

"It's a dick thing," he continued. "Sex is the most important thing in my life."

"What, more than music?"

"More than anything."

"So are your most intense emotions sexual ones?"

"No, the most devastating emotions I've experienced are feelings of depression and desolation – nothing to do with sex."

"Wow, I can't identify with that, I'm never depressed. Stressed, yes, but depressed? No. I guess I'm an intrinsically happy person."

"Lucky you."

"How does your sexuality affect your music?"

"I don't write songs about sex, but yeah, when I play it's pure sex."

Kim laughed.

"Like if there's a crowd of women on one side and a crowd of men on the other, I'll face the women."

"Wow."

"Would you like to see my guitar?"

"Okay, yes I would."

Jay disappeared out of the room. On returning he handed the instrument to her.

"You're brave. Chris won't even let me touch his in case I damage it."

He showed her how to play some chords. Kim had known how to play the guitar since she was fifteen, but it was fun to pander to his sexist assumption that she was a novice. Guys and their guitars, honestly!

"I once had a dream about you," confessed Jay, "you were in the porch of a church, playing an acoustic guitar."

"I dread to think what it meant," she laughed. "I prefer the flute. More than two feet of silver-plated perfection. What more could a girl ask for?"

"Okay, but I've just got to play this to you."

Jay launched himself into a horribly accurate imitation of Rolf Harris' version of *Stairway to Heaven*. Kim cracked up, it was too much to bear.

Jay led her to his bedroom. The curtains were already drawn against the late summer evening sunlight. This is such a cliché, she thought.

Jay leapt on the bed. Kim climbed gingerly on to the other end.

"Don't get any further away, will you," he muttered.

Kim edged closer and lay down beside him.

"Won't you feel more comfortable without your clothes on?"

Subtle, wasn't he.

"Not at the moment, no."

"I don't know whether or not you were aware of it, but I've always felt there was a degree of sexual tension between us whenever we met."

"Mmm."

"I don't know if you will remember, but once, when you were working in one of the smaller, upstairs rooms of the sixth-form college, I came in and sat opposite you..."

Kim did remember; she had been doing some physics problems at the time.

"...and I bent down to pick up a rubber. I started to stare at your legs and to fantasise about you locking the door and seducing me."

Kim crossed her eyes in the dark. Weird guy! This wasn't going to work. Her heart wasn't in it. She could be wild with Jay in the world of words, but not beyond. She wanted him, but not enough to give her desire any direction.

"Well, I've laid myself bare."

Sure, real deep stuff Jay. Why didn't he just rape her and get it over? "I know this might not sound much, Jay, but I've always been glad that you existed." She liked him for what he was, what more could she say?

Jay reached out into the dark and clasped her hand. For a fleeting moment she thrilled to his touch, and then nothing.

"Do you want to undress me, Kim?"

Images of incongruous fumbling flashed into Kim's mind. "No." She sensed a need to make a move, but felt powerless in the face of his passivity.

"Don't you want to master me?"

"Does Mandy dominate you?"

"Yes," he lied, wanting to make it easier for Kim to initiate the act.

"Why don't you make the first move for a change?"

"I don't want to. I want you to."

What was wrong with the guy? Why was he being such a wimp? What did he think she was a prostitute? Uh-oh, maybe that's what all this was, *chyripareunia gratuit.*

"Is it because I'm intellectually dominant that you want me to control you physically? Have you ever been with someone more intelligent than yourself?"

"No."

"So this is an experiment?"

"It's whatever you want it to be," he said slowly.

She got the message; he would if she would. For a brief moment the idea of making the night her own and tasting wild heaven seemed almost too wonderful. Kim could almost sense her incisors and fingernails lengthening in anticipation. She liked her pleasure spiced with pain.

But no, it wouldn't work. She had to get out of this. She would make it easy for him, she would let it be his decision.

Kim's voice, husky with tears, broke the silence. "I'm sorry Jay, I can't go through with this. My life's gone wrong so many times, I can't bear it happening again. I don't want that kind of torture."

"Maybe I can make it better."

Kim almost gasped. How could he be so crass? He hadn't even kissed her.

"What? A knight in shining armour with a long, hard, steel lance?" Her voice was flat.

"Do you want a hug?"

She didn't, but thought it best to say yes.

"Okay."

Kim nestled close to him and he held her against him. She smelt deliciously of cinnamon.

Then the real tears came. Kim hadn't been held like that by a man in a long, long time. Suddenly the pain and sorrow of the past two years welled up and out of her. No one had been there for her as she'd starved herself to near-death, and she desperately needed to be held by him. She shook within his arms.

Eventually she grew still and moved away from him, horrified to have discovered such pain so close to the surface of her being. She had thought that she was dead inside. Why on earth couldn't she have censored her hurt?

Jay sat up, "I've got a bad feeling about this," he said. "I'm going to the bathroom, I'll leave you to compose yourself."

'Wow,' thought Kim, 'I thought that I was beyond human comfort.' She got up and switched the light on.

When Jay returned he found her sitting cross-legged on the bed.

"I apologise for that outburst of gratuitous emotion," she said, smiling.

"That's okay. Do you want some coffee?"

"Mmm."

The perfect panacea.

Chapter Four

Something Sapphic

The next day Kim awoke with an unwanted but irresistible desire to see Jay again. The disturbing feeling persisted throughout the morning. She hated it, knowing and fearing its origin. Why did females always get stuck on consequence and continuity? She had to quash these sexual reverberations at any cost, so she wrote Jay a note.

> *Dear Jay,*
> *I'll look to like if looking liking move, but no more deep will I endart mine eye than your consent gives strength to let it fly.*
> *Les vrais paradis sont les paradis qu'on a perdu.*
> *K.*

She knew that it was a completely stupid thing to do, but it gave her a much needed sense of relief and release. Cast once more into the dread arena of adult emotion and desire, Kim was torn between a pre-programmed hormone high and the alienation of Jay; she chose the latter, it was more familiar territory.

Three days later she came to her senses. Time for a little damage limitation now that she was no longer at the mercy of her biochemistry. The emotional mutiny was well and truly over.

> *Hi Jay,*
> *It was just a joke.*
> *I have a bad habit of playing with words and mischief.*
> *No offence, huh?*
> *Still friends, okay?*
> *I'm sorry,*
> *Kim.*
> *PS The tears came from my wounds and not from me.*

Oh God, how should she react if she saw him again? She wouldn't know where to look. Should she smile and say hi, or should she walk cooly past him saying nothing? What if she did speak and he ignored her? That would gather the storm clouds over her for sure.

Why had she gone round to his house that evening? She had had no intention of having sex with him; she had merely been curious as to whether or not he could change her mind. On a visceral level she was thankful that nothing had happened; he might hate her, but at least her body was intact, still whole. Such physical intensity and then nothing would have been unbearable.

Time passed and Kim heard nothing from Jay. This didn't surprise her. Acting against her better judgement, she decided to go and see him. It was a Sunday, so he would probably be in. She felt compelled to ascertain the full extent of the damage she had caused.

On reaching his house she rang the bell. For once it didn't stick. There came a noise from within, then, much to her relief, the door opened.

"Hi Jay," she said, her voice quiet and her face pale and slightly nervous, "I've come to apologise for being so stupid." Kim tried to lean on the wall of the porch and stumbled.

"Are you drunk?"

"Hardly! Smell my br..." Not a good idea. "May I come in, I need to talk to you." Her hand made a small, nervous gesture.

"No," he said flatly.

Kim stared at Jay, her eyes narrowing. He stared back at her.

"Okay," she sighed. "Are you so mad at me?"

"I was, but I'm not now."

"How annoyed?" Her voice was involuntarily teasing. Shit!

"I thought you were psycho."

Kim took a deep breath. "Well, I'm not."

"Okay," he said mildly.

Kim looked Jay straight in the eye, willing him to say something more. He didn't.

"Oh well, enjoy your holiday."

Jay frowned.

"Bye," she said quietly, almost as if she were speaking to herself.

"Goodbye Kim. Mind your head on my sister's hanging basket, I know what you're like." He smiled at her.

Kim glanced upwards and saw it dangling a few inches away from her forehead. "Thanks," she grinned, then turned and walked away, her soul in tatters. Strange, she had never shed tears during her subconsciously motivated attempt at self-annihilation, so why should Jay's coldness cause her so much pain? She had made the fatal error of assuming that because Jay understood her cerebral, smart-talking side, he would understand the rest. Now, too late, she had discovered just how wrong she had been. And it was all due to the badly miscalculated risk of sending him that wretched note.

Some days later Kim awoke to find her body stiff with a long forgotten ache. She knew what it meant and reached into herself for confirmation. The fingertip came up red. Yuk! Betrayed by her own biochemistry. Just one paltry whiff of male pheromones was all it took to put her right with the moon again.

Three weeks passed. The memory of that Sunday lingered on in Kim's mind. Her image of Jay standing in the doorway, his face strangely serious and completely unyielding, with those ice-green eyes boring into her, cut her to the core. What had been in his mind? Why had he been so afraid to speak to her? Surely he had sensed her hurt.

She had no difficulty accepting his rejection, she was used to things screwing up; the anti-Midas touch. She didn't want Jay as a boyfriend, she didn't like him that much, but she did want him as a friend. She couldn't bear the thought of anyone wanting to possess her, it conflicted with her innate sense of independence. She preferred to hunt the hunter... So why was she acting like a stereotypical female victim? It wasn't like her at all.

Jay had returned from Cyprus, she had seen him in town with his cycle. The sight of him had quickened her heartbeat rate and she had found it hard to keep walking in a straight line. He had smiled at her as he cycled past, his labrador-like profile cutting into the wind, but he had said nothing. He had looked smaller than she remembered him to be.

She had to talk to him. Nothing ventured, nothing pained.

★

The Jay who answered the door appeared to be more than a little green, his previously dark eyebrows now peroxide pale.

"Hi!" piped Kim's voice, summer-bright.

"Hello."

"Are you okay? Your eyebrows look strange."

"The sun bleached them."

"Do you want to talk?"

"No." He could feel the pressure of her will upon him and it scared him.

Kim paused. Did he have to be quite so blunt? "Why not? I can be interesting."

Jay gave her a hard look, "It's like 'Do you want a Toffee Crisp?'"

"No."

"That was a rhetorical question. I just don't want to. I'm busy."

"Oh, I see. With someone or something?"

"Something. God, you're a nosy bastard."

Kim laughed. Bastard, not bitch. How very PC.

"Why Jay, you're no fun at all," she said with deliberate levity.

"Don't try and goad me." He sounded as though he meant it.

"Look, I'm sorry about those dumb notes."

"Oh, I'd forgotten about them."

But the sting remained. Boy, was she paying for her wilful stupidity.

"So why don't you want to talk?" There was death in her voice.

"I just don't." He continued to stare at her, with not a trace of emotion on his face.

"You don't know what you do to me when you're like this," she pleaded, "I feel so guilty, I didn't intend to be so damned stupid." Kim felt a sickening sensation in the pit of her stomach. She wasn't going to cry, was she?

"Don't lay a guilt trip on me." Jay's voice was low and insidiously masculine. "Look, I'm all right, you're all right." He suddenly sounded very weary.

"Same as before?"

"Okay."

Silence. The silence which meant that there was nothing more to say. Kim turned and went, all too well aware of the terrible sense of rejection she held at bay by force of will and sense of dignity. Walking past his fence, she experienced a sudden violent desire to kick it – hard – then thought better of it. Nevertheless, she recognised only too well the presence of the slow burning fuse which Jay had lit within her that night. She had better be careful it didn't blow up in their faces.

*

That night, curled up in the animal security of her bed, Kim lay still, one arm beneath the duvet, the other thrown carelessly back over her head onto a pale pink pillow, and thought long and hard about Jay. It had been a mistake to send him those notes. She now saw them for what they were; pathetic ramblings indicative of a deep sense of inner insecurity. Why couldn't she have delayed her decision to contact him for a week or so? Surely she had that much self-control. But no, she'd squandered all in one deliciously deadly moment of self-defeating weakness.

Did he really hate her? She couldn't bare the idea that he thought ill of her. She hoped that the bad feeling between them was merely transitory; all she wanted was the chance to explain how she felt. She wasn't afraid to show her emotions because she knew that she could be objective about them. She hadn't been able to say more to him, standing outside his front door, because of his manifest hostility.

Looking out of the window at the night sky, Kim wondered what Jay looked like as he slept. The thought of him inert and dreaming filled her with a peculiar sense of tenderness that tore at her heart.

She had discovered that she had developed a 'thing' for men with short, dark-blonde ponytails; this was strange as Jay had longish, butter-blonde hair. She was only too well aware of the innate superficiality of her desire; one snip and they would have meant nothing to her.

Kim turned her head languidly and stared at a picture of a male model, pinned onto her bedroom wall. He bore a dark, Italianate resemblance to Jay. God, it was ridiculous that a chiselled jawline on a thin face could have such a heart-rending effect on her. Purely visceral of course. And how delicious to have been desired by him, if only for one day.

It seemed strange that it was only since the bad feeling had developed between them that she felt free to throw aside her inhibitions and ask herself what she truly thought and felt about Jay. There was no longer any danger in such soul-searching, for if he hated her then nothing which she might do as a consequence of being aware of any feelings for him could do any more damage. She had nothing to lose, therefore the barrier had melted away.

During bad times in her recent past she had had to suppress all feeling just to survive, dealing with the pain when and where she found it. She had feared that she would never emotionally or physically want anyone ever again.

Kim fell into light sleep and dreamt that she was talking to Jay outside his door again. In the dream she reached up and touched the left side of his face. Seduction.

What did he mean to her? She had to confess that she didn't know.

*

Kim was an ardent jogger, a dedicated pavement-pounder. On some days Jay would wake with an early morning hard-on and whack himself off at the sight of her running past his window in shorts and a T-shirt, wild orange tendrils of hair – ponytail escapees – obscuring her face. She might be a shred-head Medusa, but he still wanted to nail her. Watch out coppertop!

Funny how all women ultimately proved themselves to be made out of the same material – cling film. She had been okay before that night, but now it had all gone sour. It was a shame, as he had got such a kick from her company. Some of her ideas on personal freedom were killers and she was such a feisty little female; the harder he hit, the harder she hit back. But now... well, things could never be as free and easy as they had been. He wished that she would leave him alone and stop being such a stupid little masochist; he hated it when she was so demanding.

Emotional nakedness repulsed him. He had thought that she was different, he would never have believed that she was so unstable. She had seemed so solid, more so than him at any rate. Now that she had gone into overkill mode he no longer found her kind of cake very appetising. Still waters ran deep and murky, it seemed. It was a pity as she was such a pretty little thing.

She was very intelligent, he had to give her that; light years beyond him. He had seen her as a challenge, something to figure out, but he had never expected that she would be so physically cold. It would have required a blowtorch to cut through her ice.

Why had she proved to be such a tough nut to crack? Maybe some guy had fucked her up. Well tough, he wasn't going to be anyone's emotional crutch, let her deal with her own injured innocence by herself. He wasn't going to be used in that way by her; she had lost the right to be treated with respect.

★

Chris stumbled out of his room and seized a towel from the banister just as Kim reached the top of the stairs. He looked pretty rough.

"Are you half alive or half dead?"

"Exactly," he muttered.

"I suppose you could always have 'life, but not as we know it' tattooed on your forehead."

"I'm knackered."

"Okay, I won't stay long. I just came round to drop this off."

She handed him a paperback copy of *Catch 22*.

"Uh-huh, thanks."

Chris put his towel down, then retreated into his room and got back into bed. Kim followed and sat on the end of the duvet.

"What did you think of it?" he asked.

"Brilliant, in fact I thought it was one Heller of a novel."

Chris made feeble groaning sounds.

"No, I mean it, I've had conversations like that with people. I don't know why but its mood and style reminded me of William Burroughs' *The Place of Dead Roads*, just not quite as spaced out."

"That's an interesting statement."

"Oh, why?"

"It just is."

Typical of Chris to be so needlessly enigmatic.

"How are things going with the 'Laughing Maggots'?"

"They're not, we're having an hiatus by mutual consent."

"I see. Tell me Chris, what exactly do you talk about when you're with your mates?"

"TV, music, football, cricket, life..."

"Girls?"

"To some extent, but they're not a major topic of conversation."

"Would you ever ask a girl to master you during sex?"

Chris pulled a face, "No, it would be too demeaning."

"Oh really..." Kim smiled to herself, "I'm glad you said that."

"Why? What have you been up to?"

Kim's face assumed a look of wide-eyed innocence. "Nothing."

"I bet." Chris got up and started to tune his guitar.

"Have you decided what you're going to do after you graduate?" Kim asked.

"No, I might go to Australia for a year. I've asked one of my mates if he wants to come with me, but he says he doesn't want to miss a year of *Coronation Street*."

"Wow," Kim said without much enthusiasm.

"What about you?"

"I'm thinking of doing a PGCE."

"Very D.H. Lawrence."

"Yeah, well... Oh, I know what I meant to ask you, you're studying English Literature, what was Sylvia Plath's stuff like?"

"Mmm... neurotic, self-pitying, angst-ridden, load of shite in my opinion. She was just some screwed-up American bird."

"Thanks." And thank you too, Jay.

"Why did you want to know?"

"Oh, no reason really, it's just that this guy I know said he thought my writing would be like hers."

Chris exploded into tortured laughter.

"It's not funny."

"Yes it is. So what is your writing like?"

"I don't know, it's a bit hard to categorise."

"Anne of Green Gables on acid, probably."

"Ha, ha. How little you know."

"What have you been doing with yourself recently, anything good?"

"Nothing wildly exciting. I'm seeing a university friend tomorrow, Laura. She's a junior doctor in Nottingham."

"Have fun."

"We intend to. Bye."

"Bye. See ya."

★

Kim met Laura at the station. They walked through the town to the seafront.

"How's life as a junior doc?"

"What life?" she laughed.

"That bad?"

"Worse. Half the time I think, yes, this is me, this is what I want to do with my life. The rest of the time I'm suffering from severe sleep deprivation and thinking what on earth am I doing here? I must be mad! This sucks! But, then again, I can't imagine doing anything else. I like helping people, they're the most important thing on the planet."

"What about all those male nurses running after you?"

"They don't, only the female ones," she laughed, "not that I complain about that." Kim smiled. She knew that Laura was all too well aware of her considerable bisexual allure.

They reached the beach and removed their shoes. The sand was gritty but warm beneath their feet and littered with broken shells. Laura, a sultry, olive-skinned Tori Amos, stood still and breathed in the sea air. "This is the life. Actually Kim, I have a confession to make. I used to fancy you like mad when we were at Catz."

Kim looked at her and smiled.

"You made me think of Emily Bronte's Cathy when you were on your bike, your gorgeous hair streaming out behind you."

"Somehow I don't think that Cathy was a redhead."

"Poetic licence."

"I'm flattered."

"So you should be. I could kiss you, Kim."

Kim looked uncertain. They walked on.

Walking round a grassy sand dune, Kim turned to her left and was horrified to see Jay a few metres away, rubbing lotion into the back of a prostrate female. This was too much. What a god-awful coincidence.

"Laura," she said hesitantly, "remember back there you said you wanted to kiss me..."

"Yes," Laura grinned, "why, have you changed your mind?"

"Why not? It's a beautiful day, we have sun, sand, sea..."

Kim glanced uneasily in Jay's direction. He had noticed her presence and was staring at them. Laura followed Kim's gaze, "This hasn't got anything to do with that guy over there, has it?"

Kim looked uncomfortable, "In a way, yes," she admitted, staring directly, into Laura's chocolate-brown eyes.

"Oh, I don't know about this, Kim, it's a bit sus."

"Come on Laura," Kim whispered, "he's just another guy."

"You're mad Kim, okay, but don't say I didn't warn you."

Laura took Kim's head in her hands and kissed her with finesse.

They moved away without looking back at Jay.

"I hope you realise that he'll know exactly what that was," hissed Laura.

"I do, don't worry. I just wanted to annoy him."

"So what's the story?"

"Oh, nothing really. There's not all that much to tell."

"Come on, don't be coy, Kim. Knowing you, it should be a good one."

Kim gave Laura a slightly reproachful glance. "Okay, it's like this..."

Chapter Five

Friend

Redcot looked grey and functional from the entrance to the station. Emma, very blonde and almost beautiful, emerged from the subway under the main road and walked towards Kim. Kim waved and ran to meet her.

"Hi Kim, it's wonderful to see you, how are you?"

"Fine, and you? You look tired."

"No, I'm fine too."

Kim and Emma had been buddies since university. Emma was now a biology teacher, married to an accountant called Jon.

They walked the short distance to Emma's house. She lived in a small semi with a rowan tree growing in the street outside. On opening the front door, the two girls were greeted by a small mackerel tabby.

"Oh, you have a cat! How perfect! She's adorable. What's she called?"

"Hobbs. She adopted us when we moved in."

"Why Hobbs?"

"She was fascinated by the box our kettle came in, so we named her after it."

"That's so sweet."

"Shall I put a CD on?"

"Yes please."

"Got a preference?"

"I'm not fussed, any kind of rock. I've got Jamiroquai in the blood at the moment, it's a kind of 'eco-funk'."

"I've never heard of it. Neil Young okay?"

"Sure." Kim stared at a vase of wilting red geraniums on the mantelpiece as Emma put on the CD.

"What have you been doing with yourself recently, Kim."

"Oh, I've been having driving lessons."

"How's it going?"

"So far so good, no flashing blue lights as yet."

"I passed my test when I was seventeen. I had a really strange driving instructor. He once asked me to sing whilst I was driving."

"Why?"

"I don't know, he only asked me once. I just refused to do it."

"My instructor's okay, he's really nice. He's called Arthur, but I call him Hearty Artie. He's a great guy."

Emma laughed. "Have you done any writing recently?" she said, stroking Hobbs.

"I've started a certain something which I'm going to finish – I hope. It's going quite well, almost evolving on its own in fact. I doubt anyone would ever publish it, but whatever happens, at least my typing will improve. It can't get any worse!"

Emma smiled. "I used to write poetry, but since I started teaching I've been too busy."

"I hope you don't mind me mentioning this, but you do look tired Emma, are you sure you're all right?"

"It's being a teacher... I have to work about 70 hours a week inside and outside school. I get there at 8 a.m. and stay past 6 marking and preparing lessons, and then I've more work to do when I get home."

"What are the kids like?"

"They vary a lot. Most of them are okay, but discipline is a big problem. I have a fifth-form class first thing on Monday mornings and half the lads come in hungover on cider from the night before. I can't do anything with them. I heard on the radio that people who work hard live longer; at the rate I'm going I'll live forever!"

Kim laughed. "Still, it's a challenge. Aren't they supposed to make you gain inner strength and grow as a person?"

Emma rolled her eyes. "There are some challenges that I could do without. I don't dislike teaching as such, there are lots of things about it which I enjoy. It's a wonderful experience to work with kids, because they're so full of aspirations and new ideas. Their success is the goal you work towards, it's a tremendous privilege to be able to help them realise their potential. It's the workload which gets me down. It varies so much from one school to another. Science teachers have it the hardest because there's very little opportunity to do any marking in class, they're too busy supervising practicals."

"Have you ever thought about changing your career?"

"Yes, I have actually. I'm thinking of going into educational publishing. I've been looking at some job adverts. The usual requirements are a background in education or publishing, so I may go for it."

"Well, I wish you good luck."

"How's your job-hunting going?"

"Not very well. I did have an interview with a local firm of chartered accountants offering traineeships to graduates. They interviewed four of us, I was the only one they interviewed twice. Each time, the guy who was interviewing me said 'My only concern is that this job may not be sufficiently demanding for you.' How sickening! I explained that if I didn't want the job I wouldn't have applied for it. Anyway it would have been 'sufficiently demanding', it would have been a completely fresh experience."

"That's tough."

"You can say that again. Actually, I'm thinking of going into teaching..."

"You're not."

"I know, but it's almost last resort time. The trouble is that you can't always run away from your past, sometimes it catches up with you, sinks its teeth in deep and refuses to let go."

"What do you mean?"

"I've discovered what it says on one of my academic references, something about me not being able to live a normal life in my final year because of stress. How am I expected to get a job when such a damning statement exists? I might as well have 'liability' tattooed in red across my forehead. I'm going to have to pay for driving myself too hard for the rest of my life."

"Are you all right now?"

"Recovered from my gradual slide into non-existence you mean?... Yes, I have, thanks, although my ego's slightly battered."

Kim smiled ironically. "It's so bizarre to feel caught up in a living tragedy dictated by the mistakes in my past. I hate it, I want to get out." Kim stopped speaking, having run out of steam.

"Kim," Emma said gently, "please say if you mind me asking you this, but why did you starve yourself?"

"I'm not sure, it was such a gradual process. I just began to eat less and less, I didn't intend it to happen. Thinking back, I feel nothing, no pain, no sorrow, not even regret. It happened so slowly, it seemed almost inevitable. I was a different person. It was a long, slow erosion of mind and body, I was dying within and without."

Emma put her arms round Kim and held her tight.

★

That evening they decided to go out with Jon. Kim looked at Emma's wedding photos whilst Emma applied cosmetics to her face.

"You look beautiful in these shots, you're so photogenic, you lucky thing."

"Don't, I look hideous."

"As if!... You make me feel really guilty. I haven't used make-up since I was a teenager when I used to put blue eye-shadow on my lips. I can't even pluck my eyebrows because it creates freckles just above my eyes."

"You're okay, with your colouring you don't need it."

"I don't suppose there's much point, people don't see my face, just my red hair. Mind you that's probably a blessing."

"You're too hard on yourself."

"You think so? I like my eyes, lips and legs, but I think the jury's out on the rest. It's okay for you, men virtually fall at your feet wherever you go."

"Don't exaggerate. Besides, I don't trust good-looking men, they're too used to getting their own way. Anyway, talking of man-eaters, how's Laura?"

"Immersed in medicine, but as sultry and stunning as ever. What was her record? Eight minutes on from meeting a guy, or girl, and furniture rolls."

"That's our Laura."

★

The trio headed for a pub.

Once inside and sipping grapefruit juice with ice, Kim was overcome by a wave of facetiousness. "Jon, do you think it's possible for a man to like a woman as a friend and not desire her? I mean, can a man like a woman who he doesn't find sexually attractive?"

"I don't know, I guess so."

"But wouldn't sex inevitably get in the way and ruin everything?"

"Not necessarily." He gave the impression of being deliberately vague, but Kim wasn't going to be beaten.

"Do you know of any instances where it hasn't?"

He was at a loss. Ha! Just as she had expected.

"And what do you think of men who stick pictures of tacky blondes on their walls?"

At first Jon refused to be drawn. Eventually Kim got her answer.

"They should get back into the real world and start talking to people."

"Thank you."

"Is that what you wanted?"

Kim looked at him sharply. "It'll do."

★

The following day, Kim and Emma drove out into the Derbyshire countryside in Emma's car.

"Have you got a boyfriend yet, Kim?"

"No, but I've got to know a guy I went to sixth-form college with quite well, or at least better than I used to."

"What's he like?"

"Not tall, long, bottle-blonde hair, a bit like a 5 foot 4 Barbie doll I suppose. Quite intelligent, plays the guitar in a band."

"Can he play properly?"

"I think so."

"Is he nice?"

"He can be, but..."

"But what?"

"I don't think he likes me very much at the moment."

"What happened?"

"He tried to seduce me, but I refused to play ball... then I sent him this dumb note."

"Oh Kim, you didn't."

"I know, I know. He already has a girlfriend. He was so blasé about being unfaithful to her. They've been together for years on and off, so he must care about her. He said that she would leave him if she found out about the times he's cheated on her, but my impression is that she hasn't got the guts to do it."

"Sounds like he's using her."

"Maybe. She's less intelligent than he is. He told me he'd made it clear to her that he'd never marry her or have kids or anything. He isn't a stereotypical male bastard, he's just honest with himself about what he wants."

"What a sensitive guy. So what's she like?"

"Pretty bland, bit of a nonentity really. Nice though, sweet face, light brown hair, likes Metallica. I hate making her sound so pathetic, but I'm basically repeating what he's told me. She's very dependent on him."

"Do you still miss Simon?"

"Yes, yes I do." Kim frowned. "He was such a guy... I'd never slept with anyone before him. He made me feel so safe; I knew he would never reject me, I could sense it in his voice and eyes."

"I know what you mean, Jon can be so loving."

"I remember when I first set eyes on him in the Mill Lane lecture rooms, something shook me to the core, he had a sense of grace about him... Oh well, nothing lasts forever. He's an actuary in London now. We still write to each other, but it's not the same."

★

The next day, Emma drove Kim to the station. On the way there, Kim posted a picture postcard to Jay. 'Dear Jay, I know you don't give a damn, but tomorrow is another day, K.'

Emma waited with Kim until the train arrived.

"I'm really glad you came, you seem so much happier."

"I am, probably because I've had more time to be human recently."

"Well goodbye and good luck."

"You too, it's been wonderful to see you again. Bye... and don't work too hard, Emma."

"Easier said than done. Remember to keep in touch."

"I will, bye."

Kim got onto the train and closed the door.

Chapter Six

Pen and Ink

It was raining when Jay spotted Kim walking home from the station. "Oh no," he breathed, "it's Agent Orange."

Her head was uncovered and her hair, the colour of apricot jam, was dripping wet. Typical of Kim not to be deterred by the downpour, he thought. How come she had such a good tan? Weren't redheads supposed to be fair-skinned? Maybe it was because she had brown eyes.

Jay was cycling fast, his face partially hidden by a dark hood. He hoped that she wouldn't recognise him. No such luck! He watched as she stared quizzically at him for a moment, then saw a smile break out on her face. In spite of himself, he reciprocated, stopped, and got off his cycle.

"Hi! How are things with you?"

"Fine." He sounded defensive and her face fell.

"Your eyebrows look better, you looked slightly ill when I last saw you."

Jay stared at her, saying nothing, his lime-green eyes fixed firmly on her face.

"Would you like to talk?" she asked, her voice little more than a whisper.

"Definitely not," he replied flatly.

Before Kim had time to respond, he got back onto his bike and sped away. "Bye," she called after his retreating form. 'Wow,' she thought, 'that was brief.'

How could something so good turn so sour? Why was it so horribly easy for male-female friendships to snarl up? She knew that sex could be destructive, but who would have thought that almost-sex could be just as devastating? If only Jay would loosen up and stop taking everything so seriously; surely she didn't stress him out that much. She had thought they were really good friends and that there was some degree of kindness and humanity in Jay. Had she been wrong all along or was she just experiencing the flip side of his personality? Whatever it was, she wished that he would snap out of it PDQ.

★

Kim had applied for the post of mathematics teacher at Blackwood Hall, a private co-educational school located in the wilds of Shropshire. A PGCE wasn't a legal requirement for teaching in the private sector.

Kim was picked up from the station, together with another candidate, by the school minibus. They introduced themselves to each other.

"Hello, I'm Alan Giles."

"Hi. I'm Kim Murray. I guess we're in competition."

"Looks like it."

At the school, they were met by the school's secretary and Kim discovered that Mr Giles was Dr Giles.

"So you're a Ph.D., I might as well give up now!" exclaimed Kim in mock horror.

"Oh, I don't know, it could prove to be a disadvantage."

"I don't see why it should, unless it makes you more expensive. What are you doing in secondary education with qualifications like that?"

"I've just finished an overseas contract. Since coming back to Britain, I've found that the structure of higher education has changed completely. I no longer feel that there's a place for me."

There were two other candidates, both male, one a thickset rugger-bugger type, the other a dark Adonis. Kim was younger and at least a foot shorter than each of the three men. Things were not looking good, she decided. However, she wasn't going to give up without a fight.

The formal interviews with the headmaster and the head of maths went well. Afterwards she talked to the rest of the staff, as did the other interviewees. Kim was the only one to befriend the school dog, a small grey bundle called Misty.

At the end of the day the headmaster informed them that it would be very difficult for him to choose between them, he would have to resort to the "third criterion". They would be notified of the final decision within a week.

Kim and Dr Giles left on the same train.

"What do you think is meant by the 'third criterion'?" mused Kim.

"I don't know, it sounded a bit painful to me."

"I wonder who will get it?"

"Time will tell."

Kim smiled, "What did you study for your PhD?"

"Viscous fluids."

"I bet that was a drag," she quipped.

He laughed. "Why do you want to be a teacher?"

"I don't," she replied, "it's a last resort. What did you think of the staff?"

"Slightly eccentric."

"Mmm, it must be the splendid isolation."

"I'm going to get a coffee, would you like one?"

"No, thanks, I'm fine."

Left on her own, Kim took a writing pad and pen from her bag and scribbled a note intended for Jay. She wasn't going to give up on him.

> *Hi Jay!*
>
> *I don't know if anyone's dazed and confused, but I hate communication breakdown, especially if kindness gets trampled underfoot. Oh well, I suppose it's nobody's fault but mine.*
>
> *Take care/ gefahrlich leben,*
> *K*

Kim parted company from Dr Giles when she changed trains at Shrewsbury. Before she caught her connection she posted the letter in a postbox standing just outside the station.

⋆

Kim heard nothing from Jay. She was afraid that his perception of her had become badly distorted and that he was storing up a whole heap of resentment against her. She wasn't sure of what she felt for him, but something in his gaze touched her to the quick, that much she was prepared to admit to herself. They had seemed to be in 'synch', she could be herself with him in ways that she couldn't with other people; she could be bad with him.

If only she could regain his trust. She didn't think that anything would be gained by confronting him directly, she could imagine only too well what would happen:

I think you may have misjudged me and my actions.

I don't think so.

Look, I'm not saying that I don't have flaws, I do, probably near-fatal ones, but they're not the ones you think I have.

I'm not interested.

Kim wondered if Jay appreciated just how lucky he was to possess the luxury of callousness. Did he find her persistence a real turn-off? She didn't want to be the stereotypical female victim, yet at night, in bed, she would sob out her soulful soliloquies of spiritual isolation. She didn't have to heed the hurt, but then again there was an inherent danger in being comfortably numb. She didn't want to become insensitive to human hurt; you got burnt when you stepped into the flames, regardless of whether or not you felt the pain.

Sometimes Jay would pass Kim in the street. He would ignore her even if she called out to him. This would sting, and she would phone him in the hope that he would speak to her and allow her the opportunity to heal the damage. He rarely answered and on the occasions when he did pick up the receiver, he would slam it down as soon as he heard her voice. God, she hated the impasse. She wondered if he had any idea just how much his unrelenting hostility hurt her; she felt as though all the warmth in her life was slowly draining away.

★

A week later Kim received a letter from Blackwood Hall. She hadn't got the job, but the letter was encouraging.

Dear Miss Murray,

Thank you for coming to the interview for the post of teacher of mathematics at Blackwood Hall. I did enjoy meeting you and I confirm that this particular selection has been a most difficult appointment, for all the candidates could so easily have fulfilled the post.

I felt that you have the potential to be a great teacher and if we had a bigger department I would have been prepared to take the risk of appointing you and seeing that potential grow into reality. With a department of just two, you will appreciate however, that a much greater responsibility is placed upon each member of staff and it is with sadness, therefore, that I have to advise you that I am not able to appoint you to this post.

I do believe that you will make a great teacher and I would recommend that you do take a PGCE course, for this will give you all the practice that you need to begin to hone your skills and release your full potential.

I wish you every success for the future.
Yours sincerely,
L.M. Taylor

The letter made Kim feel optimistic; she had apparently made a good impression. Yes, she thought, I've made my decision, I will become a teacher, I'll apply to the GTTR to do a PGCE. There will always be a demand for teachers, especially maths teachers, and it will be good to be part of something. Emma would think she was mad but it was probably harder for Emma, having to arrange and supervise practicals on top of everything else.

It would be tough, but she was ready to give it her best shot. Yes, she had made her decision, she would go for it.

Phew! Making plans for life always left Kim feeling 'hyper', as though she had OD'd on caffeine. Compelled to go for a run to dissipate her excess energy, she changed into shorts and T-shirt.

Out on the streets, Kim felt incredible; a lithe, swift-legged creature with muscles of steel. She sped along the pavement on her ballerina legs with hardly any physical effort, savouring the crunch of her trainers on the concrete and the early evening smell of onions frying.

She hadn't felt this good in a long, long time.

Oh God! Kim's heart almost stopped. She could see Jay in front of her, on foot for once and wearing a pink hat that clashed horribly with his dyed hair. Oh no, thought Kim. She slowed her pace down to a brisk walk and headed towards the inevitable. Maybe she would strike lucky this time.

"Hi," she breathed as she reached him. Jay stared at her for a moment, then turned his head away and walked on, saying nothing. His rejection hit her like a blast of ice-cold air. Pig! It doesn't cost anything to be friendly, he could at least have said hello... what I wouldn't give to separate that banana-blonde midget from his skin. Kim, fuming, continued her run. Crossing the road, she came into sight of two workmen digging a ditch in the street. One of them bent over as she approached and ran his hand through his short blonde hair, "Howdy ma'am," he drawled in a fake American accent as she ran past. Kim smiled in spite of herself.

The incident with Jay hung over her like a cloud when she got home. She headed straight for the shower to wash the sweat off her skin. The cool water felt good on her hot body, but her mind continued to buzz. She would call Jay to see if he could be reasonable over the telephone. She had no clear idea what she was going to say, but what the hell.

Kim dialled the number. A low, masculine voice answered, but it was no good, her nerve failed her and she hung up. Rats!

She was halfway up the stairs when the phone rang. Kim hesitated, then dashed down to answer it.

"Hello," she said brightly, into the receiver.

"Who's this speaking?" It was Jay's voice.

"Why?" she replied in a slightly suspicious tone.

"So, it's like that is it, Kimberley? I thought it was you who hung up on me. Well now I'm going to do the same to you, to get you back."

He hung up.

Kim recoiled from the phone. She felt crushed. How could he be so childish? And why on earth did he call her Kimberley? Why so formal, would she have to call him James in future?

Kim couldn't rest. She had to make peace with Jay and put an end to this comedy of errors. She refused to follow him along the path of hate. She would write to him again; it was worth a try, she couldn't make it worse.

> Hi Jay!
>
> I guess that by writing this note I'm giving myself a lot of rope with which to hang myself. I have a horrible feeling that I'm handing you the ultimate macho fantasy on a plate, that of having a girl who

you can hurt at no personal cost to yourself. But I figure, so what? Things are rarely as simple as they seem.

I apologise for any negative feeling that I may have caused you. I rang because it hurt when you ignored me for no good reason. I just want us to be friends again.

Ciao,
Kim

Jay didn't reply. Surprise, surprise. Kim hadn't expected him to. She had given him the knife and the opportunity to stick it in and twist. And guess what, he had done just that.

Why did Jay's coldness hurt her so much? Maybe it was because all her past hurts were connected and, like dominoes standing in a circle, it only required one to fall to cause the rest to topple. Perhaps she should be grateful to Jay for triggering this gush of emotion. She had been dead to all feeling for too long following her flight into near self-perdition. It had been a long, slow abrasion of the spirit: now, at last, she was feeling the pain.

Yet, all the same, she was dangerously close to not being hurt by him at all. It would be so easy to dismiss it from her thoughts and forget him. She wanted life, she wanted pain. She didn't possess too much emotion, she had too little, but she had made the mistake of showing more than she should have. It was that which had made Jay flip. She'd been too intense.

It would have hurt her too much not to let herself be hurt; she didn't want that, she needed the pain to find herself again. Jay was essential to the process. She knew that she was going about it the wrong way, but she didn't know what else to do. She refused to give up on him.

She sent him a Christmas greeting. She didn't expect him to reciprocate, but she was determined not to sink to his level. Wounds do heal with time, he might like her again, someday. Taking a piece of thick, white paper, she sketched a good likeness of a sprig of holly with a soft, dark pencil. On the other side she wrote the message:

Happy Saturnalia Jay,
Peace, goodwill, whatever.
K.

Chapter Seven

Terrorist

Jay had cut her in the street. He had hung up on her. He hadn't even sent her a Christmas card. With black humour, Kim realised that the prognosis wasn't very good. However, she remained convinced that Jay's actions were grounded on misinformation and misinterpretation. Kim was the eternal optimist, and she had always seen rejection as a challenge. She gave him a call.

"Could I speak to Jay please?" She sounded unsure of the response, as well she might after such a long silence, her phone calls unanswered. "Who is that?" A woman's voice.

"Kim."

"All right."

Distant voices: "Well are you coming?", "Yeah, all right." She could hear her heart thumping in her chest.

"Hello," It was Jay. The masculine depth in his voice stirred something in her.

"Hi, Jay. This is just a friendly call," she took a deep breath and licked her lips. Please don't let him hang up. "I know you have some hostility towards me and I'd like to know why, please." Her voice sounded strained.

"What?"

Kim repeated her question and laughed nervously.

"Oh, all right... it's because you've been silly, terrorising me."

"Terrorising you?" That was the limit! "How?"

"By sending me those notes."

"Which notes? Surely not the Christmas card?"

"Well, no. That was just a piece of paper anyway."

Kim swallowed. "I wasn't trying to terrorise you, Jay. I'm very sorry if I created that misconception."

Jay laughed, "All right." Did he mean it? Wow! She would never have guessed that he suspected her of having malignant designs on him.

"Bye."

"See ya, Kim."

Kim hung up. At least she knew the truth now. She supposed she ought to be grateful for that, and that he hadn't hung up. But to be accused or terrorising him, that was too much! Kim didn't know whether to laugh or cry. She fell onto the sofa and proceeded to do both simultaneously until her ribs ached. Who would have thought he had been nursing such paranoid delusions?

*

Kim heard a knock on her bedroom door. It opened and Chris walked in looking uncharacteristically human.

"Hi Chris. What, up so early? Wow, it must be all of ten o'clock. Nothing wrong, is there?"

"Very funny. No, I just came to see you."

"Thanks, how did the term go?"

"Okay, I've finished my dissertation. I got a 2:1 for it."

"Hey, well done. I'm really pleased for you... how's the girlfriend situation?"

"I've been too busy working, I've had to make do with a series of one night stands."

"I see."

"What have you been up to?"

"You'll never believe this. Some guy actually accused me of terrorising him!"

"Why? What did you do?"

"Nothing much. I wrote him a letter using Led Zep song titles."

"So?"

"He likes their music. I may have committed sacrilege in his eyes."

"What? That corny cock rock! You know some strange people."

"Tell me about it. He's just a paranoid little wimp... what a victim, accusing a girl of terrorising him!"

Chris laughed.

"What's worse, he even used to fantasise about me."

Kim's voice resonated with genuine disgust.

"He fantasised about you? That confirms it, the guy needs help."

"Thanks Chris... By the way, I've got an interview at Oxford tomorrow."

"What for?" He sounded unusually interested.

"PGCE in maths."

"Good on you." He sounded as though he meant it.

"Thanks. How goes the band?"

"Okay. No, better than that, actually. We've had some really good jamming sessions recently; we've got six songs down on tape and Mark's getting a new guitar – an Epiphone."

"That's great. Keep plugging it... you're only truly alive when you're doing something creative and original."

"Very T.S. Eliot."

"Really?" She sounded dubious. "May I hear some of your songs sometime?"

"As it happens, I do have the tape on me. I can't let you borrow it as it's going to be doing the rounds shortly, but I'll let you listen to it now if you like."

"Sure I would, thanks, I promise not to laugh, at least not too hard."

"Thanks," he said drily, then slotted the tape into her cassette player and switched on.

Kim waited in anticipation... guys' voices near the mike, snatches of conversation – authentic demo stuff... and then the music began.

Kim was immediately impressed. In fact she loved it; it sounded fresh, yet incredibly polished. It made her think of Ocean Colour Scene.

"Hey Chris, it's brilliant, it really is..." She laughed. "Wow, it's really good, I'm not just saying that..." She made more appreciative noises.

"You really ought to do something with this, it's frighteningly good and it's very rare that I like something the first time I hear it."

Chris let a wide grin creep slowly across his face.

*

After Chris had left, Kim went for a walk, wearing a loose grey shirt over an indigo T-shirt, her lithe legs clad in dark blue leggings. Her mind was soon elsewhere, lost in the land of Red Hot Chilli Peppers videos and *Zen and the Art of Motorcycle Maintenance*. Robert Pirsig was so incredibly easy to trash. Just as she was thinking, 'Well he could always have opened the car window', ARGHHH! A Neanderthal shout cut through her stream of thought and her body jerked backwards in shock. She felt as though she'd been shot in the back. Colours flooded through her mind, "God!" she breathed. Opening her eyes, she focused on a red car which had just passed her. Jay was sitting in the back, staring at her fixedly. She glared at him, then looked away.

Ha! She looked as though she was having an orgasm. Shafted by his shout. He loved it.

★

The interview at the Department of Education in Oxford went well for Kim, despite her turning up half an hour late after missing her connection at Birmingham. Afterwards she walked directly back to the station. She had time to spare before her train arrived, and a couple of ten pence pieces in her pocket. It was fate; she'd call Jay, just to remind him of her existence.

"Hi!", her voice was full of light.

"Oh, hello." He sounded pleased, maybe he hadn't recognised her voice, or maybe he was thinking of yesterday.

"This is a call from Oxford, believe it or not."

"Oh yeah?" His voice was wary.

"I've just had an interview at the university, so if you want to put a hex on me for making you think I was terrorising you, now is the time to do it."

"How did it go?"

"I don't know. You never can tell. I'll hear in about a week."

"Well how well do you think you did?" His voice was non too friendly.

"Hmm, well at one point one of the two interviewers turned to the other one and said, 'That was a good answer. I thought that was a difficult question.' So I suppose that's a hopeful sign."

The pips sounded. "Bye," she said and hung up.

Chapter Eight

Breathe

Kim was flying high. She felt healthier in her mind and body than she had done at any previous time in her life. She had been accepted for a place at Oxford to study for a PGCE starting in September, and her writing was coming on better than ever. She felt able to be herself wherever she was, suddenly she felt so alive, she had never felt so good inside. Her thoughts and emotions were in synch, devoid of all self-conscious self-censorship. She was light years away from the Kim who had starved herself in an attempt to prevent herself from thinking and feeling too much. She now had the existential sang-froid and inner sense of security to cut herself free from the lies of her past without a qualm. Life was getting better every day. Kim went running more often than ever. She had a whole new physical confidence, she felt at one with her body. She was eating less. Somehow she never seemed hungry; besides, she didn't want the food to weigh her down.

Jay was being friendly to her again, although things were still not as good as before. Still, at least he was answering her telephone calls.

"Hi Jay, I thought I would call, as I've just finished reading *Zen and the Art of Motorcycle Maintenance*, or rather, as it should be called, *'Zen and the Art of Mental Masturbation'*."

She heard him laugh on the other end of the line. "Oh yeah," he said.

"Yes, you once told me that I should read it."

"That was last summer, wasn't it?"

"I didn't think much of it, the guy understands nothing about the true nature of science or mathematics."

"Yeah, I thought it was superficial shit."

"Why did you recommend it to me, then?"

"I can't remember. I'm more into Nietzsche..."

"You're not, are you? The guy was mad, virtually everything he wrote lacks balance, it's either OTT or over-generalised! He obviously had no concept of the distinction between universal and existential quantifiers."

Jay was silent.

"Give me Sartre any day. Nietzsche was to philosophy, what Peter Greenaway is to aesthetics."

"Umm, is that the only reason you called?"

"Eh... yes, it was a spur of the moment thing... So how are things with you?"

Jay said nothing.

"I mean musically," Kim blurted out into the silence.

"Not too good. A bit slow actually, but things are still moving."

"Good. How does it feel when you play your guitar in front of people who actually want to hear you?"

"I'm not sure that they do. I can't really describe it without sounding trite."

A pause. Kim racked her brain for something to say. She needn't have bothered, the silence said it all. Finally it was Jay who spoke. "Sorry, I don't want to be rude, but my mate's here, we're watching the footy."

"That's okay, thanks for talking to me," she said, letting her hand play with the telephone cord.

"Um." He hung up.

★

A few days later, Kim decided to call on Jay. Jay's sister, Helen, opened the door. She was a pretty girl with short brown hair.

"Hi. Is Jay in?"

Helen gave Kim a startled look. "Jay moved out at the weekend, he and the rest of the band have gone to Manchester."

"Did he leave an address?"

"Yes, come in and I'll write it down for you."

Kim followed Helen inside. She scribbled something on a piece of paper and handed it to Kim. "Do you want to leave a message in case he rings?"

"Eh, yes. Tell him I wish him good luck and that I've got a place at Oxford for September."

"Okay. Bye."

"Bye, and thanks."

Kim left.

Wow! He had gone. Kim felt stunned and oddly relieved. Where did that come from? she wondered. Perhaps it was because he was no longer around to judge her. Walking home, her mind felt as though it was filled with a strange sort of energy, probably an aegis against the dread thought that she might never see Jay again. Why hadn't he said goodbye? She must have missed him by a couple of days. Was his callousness calculated or casual? She had to keep all sense of hurt and emptiness at bay. Nevertheless, she anticipated that her blood would come early this month.

Jay could never be more than a friend to her, but she still didn't want to lose contact with him. She decided to write to him.

> *Dear Jay,*
>
> *Hi! I heard that you'd moved so I thought I would write to wish you good luck. Now I'm going to be very boring and talk about myself.*
>
> *I've got a place at Keble College, Oxford to do a PGCE in September. I suppose it was inevitable that I would end up as a teacher. I think that I'll like it at Oxford, it's a lot like Cambridge, the principal difference being that the roads are wider and busier.*
>
> *In the meantime, I'm looking for lab work. I did a term as a NatSci at Cambridge before I defected to the Mathmos, so I'm well-versed in the art of analytical chemistry.*
>
> *On the wilder side of life, I've got a huge purple and yellow bruise on my right arm, the consequence of a series of encounters on and with a tumbling mat. It was my own fault, I made the near-fatal error of saying 'Can I counter? I think it looks easier' – big mistake!*
>
> *I've been playing my flute a lot. I've mastered Jamiroquai's Manifest Destiny. The only tricky bit is the breathing, if you get it wrong you faint.*
>
> *Good luck,*
>
> *Kim*

Kim had been in two minds as whether or not she should write to Jay, fearing that her persistence would irritate him. She doubted that he would reply, but she couldn't bear the thought of losing contact with him. She had felt compelled to do something. It was ridiculous not to be friends when they got on so well, simply because of a stupid misunderstanding. Even after the outbreak of hostility between them she had been able to make him laugh on the telephone. If he still found her funny and interesting, she didn't see why he should continue to be so cold. She didn't mind if she didn't matter more to him than the things she said; she preferred it that way.

After posting the letter, Kim returned home and made herself a coffee. A wave of loneliness passed through her as the water boiled, and she broke down. Crouching on the tiled floor with her head on her knees, hugging her legs with her arms, she sobbed and sobbed. Why hadn't he said goodbye when she phoned him? It felt as though he had drawn a bow very slowly and deliberately over her few remaining unbroken heartstrings.

Jay received the letter the following day. That night he had troubled sleep. He dreamt that he was playing his guitar in a dark, smoky club, but no one could hear him. Then he saw Kim in a white dress, dancing with a tall, blonde woman wearing black leather. Their bodies were closely entwined and they were kissing. He threw his guitar onto the floor and it broke in two. As he stared at his smashed instrument, someone clapped him on the back and suddenly he felt icy cold. Turning round he found Kim standing behind him with a scarlet stain on her dress. "You've got blood on you," he heard himself say. She smiled at him, "Don't worry, it isn't mine."

On emerging from the dream, Jay lay awake for some time, staring into the darkness. His mind was cocaine-clear and it resonated with thoughts of Kim; the imprint of her letter was still on him. The bitch haunted him wherever he went. Why couldn't she just leave him alone? Her unrelenting persistence oppressed him. What was up with her? What did she want from him? Why didn't she just get a life and get out of his?

★

Kim remained on a low for some days after learning that Jay was gone. She hated the nagging sense of emptiness which she felt. Suddenly her life seemed to be so hollow, and the world a colder, more hostile place. Why did she feel like this? It wasn't as if he had played an active part in her life. He hadn't even been very friendly towards her over the last few months. So why did she miss his presence so much? Was it merely dismay at having lost the opportunity to make peace with him properly that gnawed at her insides day and night? Or was it something more? What were her true feelings for him? She had become adept at making light of her hurt over the last few years, maybe dangerously so. It was a good pragmatic device to ease her pain at moments of desolation, but still, pain did serve to warn and protect. It would be foolish to ignore it in all instances.

But all the same, why should one man have such a devastating effect on her? Did she really not know the answer or was she simply afraid of the truth? She just wasn't sure. There was something about him which inspired her, she did acknowledge that much, but she was reluctant to contemplate what lay beneath that surface feeling or consider to what extent the attraction was animal rather than spiritual. He did make her smile though, she had to admit that. Maybe that was sufficient reason to justify not wanting to lose him.

Chapter Nine

Catharsis

Kim's PGCE course was due to begin in mid-September with a two week period of observation in a primary school. Kim had written to the headmaster, Mr Moore, of the local primary school to obtain permission to undertake this part of her course at his school. He had written back to Kim to assure her that that he could arrange something to fit the requirements of her course, and to invite her to come and be shown around the school.

Mr Moore was an extremely small man, but he appeared to be a dedicated and efficient headmaster. Kim wondered if his lack of inches had led him into primary education, the poor man was even shorter than herself. The visit made a strong impression on Kim; at last she had something solid to look forward to.

Walking home, Kim passed the house which Jay had used to share with his sister and which was now occupied by his sister alone. Glancing up at one of the windows, Kim was startled to see a blonde figure looking out at the sky. Jay! He must have returned for a few days. Thank God. She had another chance to make peace with him. What luck!

The following morning, Kim phoned Jay.

"Hello?" It was his voice. He sounded sleepy, but in a good mood.

"Hi Jay, is that really you?"

A pause. "Sorry, who is that?"

Sugar! Couldn't he hear her?

"Jay, can you hear me?" She could hear him clearly.

"Is anyone there?" He sounded perfectly normal... too normal.

"Is this a joke, Jay?"

There was another pause, then he hung up.

"Oh very funny Jay, you're so original."

Kim wasn't going to give up that easily. She rang again and let the phone ring for some time, but he refused to bite. Time for a more direct approach. Kim opened the front door and stepped out into the street.

When she got to his house, she rang the bell immediately and waited... and rang the bell and waited... and rang the bell and waited... and gave up.

Why was he doing this to her? Why did he insist on punishing her? If he hadn't wanted to speak to her, why hadn't he simply said so over the telephone? How could he be so hateful? Didn't he have a conscience? He had liked her once, so why did he hate her now?

Kim walked away, her eyes glazed with tears. There was one hope left through; if she called on Jay that evening, sometime after six, his sister would probably be in. Surely she wouldn't leave Kim stranded on the doorstep. It was worth a try.

As Kim got ready for the big event, a white heat swept through her, leaving her skin deathly pale but hot to the touch. Her stomach churned as she brushed her hair, yet she felt perfectly calm in her mind. She would go to the slaughter like a wolf in lamb's clothing.

On reaching Jay's house she rang the bell without a moment's hesitation. She heard movement from within and then the door opened. It was Jay. At last! He had a toothbrush in his mouth and he was naked to the waist. His hair had been scraped back into a ponytail; he looked as though he was getting ready to go out for the evening.

Kim smiled, "Hi, I'm sorry to call at this inopportune moment, but I really need to talk to you."

Jay removed the toothbrush from his mouth, "I've got to catch a bus in ten minutes." His voice sounded neutral. How could he be so cool when he had behaved so badly towards her?

"That's okay, what I have to say won't take five minutes."

There was a quiet note of urgency in her tone.

"Okay, wait here, I'll be with you in three minutes."

"No kidding?" Hope crept into her voice.

"No." He sounded almost friendly.

Jay closed the door and Kim breathed a long sigh of relief. At last she could relax. She leant against the brick wall and closed her eyes. Her mind was blank. She supposed she should be planning what she was going to say to him when he reappeared, but for some reason it didn't seem to matter any more. For the moment, it was enough for Kim to savour her reprieve. She had finally gained the chance to straighten out the mess of the last eight months. God, it seemed like an age. A red car on the opposite side of the road drove away and Kim watched it as it disappeared out of view.

A short while later, Jay reappeared. "I'm going to the bus stop, we can talk on the way." He shot off and Kim followed.

"I'd better explain why I seem to have been cultivating a spirit of perseverance." Kim's voice was light and slightly wistful. She felt high despite all the past hurt, because at last she had the chance to make things right. "Please talk in English." He sounded as though he was in a good mood.

Kim relaxed, this was going to be far easier than she had anticipated. "Okay. It's just that after that day last summer, I was afraid you would hate me. That's why I sent you all those notes, I wanted to repair the damage I'd caused. Of course, me being me, I managed to achieve what I'd set out to avoid by the very means I used to avoid it." She bit her lip, sensing the unconscious intensity in her voice.

Jay stared at her. "Well, let me give you a hint. If you want to clear something up with someone, don't go nuts and start leaving them weird messages."

"I know, I'm sorry, I was simply trying to set this twisted thing straight... Anyway, why did you pretend that you couldn't hear me when I phoned this morning?" There was an edge of bitterness in her tone.

"I was sleepy, I'd been out all night and I'd only just got in."

"You could have said that you were tired, or busy or something."

"Yeah, well you would probably have asked me to define 'busy'."

Kim was silent. He was right.

"And then you kept on ringing, eighty-two times to be exact. I was quite disappointed, I would have expected a nice round number like one hundred from a mathematician like you."

He had actually been counting?

At that moment, Helen passed by them with one of her friends in tow. Jay made a 'high five' gesture and Helen reciprocated. Kim experienced a pang; she wished that she had a brother.

Jay turned back to Kim, all teeth and large, wild eyes. He was so gloriously sexy. "I don't hate you, Kim, but you scared me. You were so intense. I thought we were really good mates, then you went psycho."

"Yes, I thought we were... are really good mates, too," she said, her eyes shining.

"I seemed to see you everywhere I went. It was as if you knew my every movement. I felt that you were stalking me."

"I wasn't! I just wanted the opportunity to talk to you. I knew that there was a big misunderstanding going on... I wanted to get rid of it." It was strange that she should want him when she knew she didn't really fancy him. It must be a power-play thing, she surmised.

"Are you sure there wasn't an element of stalking?" he asked, concentrating hard on her.

"No... no, of course not. I can understand how it might have seemed that way, but it wasn't my intention... I thought you knew me better than that."

"Why did you write that stuff in French?"

"It was a quote, I thought you would be able to understand French."

"Well, I wasn't. You should have put what it meant in English."

"But that would have defeated the purpose, I was trying to be poetic. Did you understand what gefahrlich leben meant?"

"No."

"I thought you would, it's your beloved Nietzsche. It means 'live dangerously'. You always used to say 'take care' whenever you said goodbye to me, which is the antithesis of 'live dangerously'. I thought you might appreciate the asymmetry."

They reached the bus stop. There was no one else there.

"I noticed that if I said 'hi', you wouldn't ring, yet if I didn't, you would," continued Jay, "I mean, to be hurt by that is way OTT."

"I thought that if you didn't say anything, you did so deliberately, to get at me."

"And then, I'd been in Manchester for only a few days when I got a letter from you. It was too much. I know a lot of people round here better than I know you and I didn't tell them where I was going."

"I know," said Kim, blushing.

"Okay, I'll admit it. I'm a twenty-three year-old man and you scared me. I was fucking frightened to death. You're very intelligent, and you hear of people like that turning into psychopaths. I thought it was my turn to fall victim to one of them."

Wow, he really was paranoid. What would have happened if she *had* tried to terrorise him? He'd probably have had a nervous breakdown. Kim knew that she was no psychopath, but she was beginning to wonder whether Jay was becoming more than a little psychotic.

"I think that's stretching things a bit far," she said eventually.

"I don't, I was fucking terrified. I didn't know what you might do. When I saw you come round just now I thought 'Oh no, what does she want?' I was going to go out and punch you."

Kim laughed, "I'm sorry, I didn't want it to happen like that."

Jay was smiling back at her. The old rapport was still as strong as ever. She loved it when he was like this. Pity he wasn't taller. She might even have fancied him if he hadn't been quite so vertically-challenged.

"I couldn't bear the thought that if ever we met on the astral plane, you would kick dust in my eyes."

He laughed.

"So what are you doing at the moment?" she asked.

"You mean 'now generally' or 'now specifically'?"

"Now generally."

"I'm going around with the band, playing in different towns, trying to get noticed. We're using Manchester as a base."

Jay stared at his watch, "I'm dead if I've missed this bus."

Kim hoped he had. She was enjoying herself too much. She didn't want a bus to turn up and spoil it.

"Do you like 'Cast'?" she asked.

Jay looked surprised, "God, I wondered what you were talking about for a moment, I thought we were talking about the bus... You mean did they rip off 'Oasis' or the 'Beatles'?"

"Actually, 'Tell it like it is' sounds like 'Hotel California' and 'Reflections' rips off R.E.M.'s 'Circus Envy'."

Jay smiled down at Kim with a strange look in his eyes. She turned to see if the bus was coming and as she did Jay suddenly put his arm around her shoulder and kissed her hard on the left cheek.

"Good luck!" he said as he released her. Stunned, she looked up. The bus was coming. "Thanks," she mumbled and walked away, feeling very light-headed.

Wow! She hadn't expected that.

Chapter Ten

And More

Kim remained on a high for the rest of the evening. She felt charged with a sense of confidence and energy which electrified every fibre of her being. How sweet those fifteen minutes with Jay had been. She was vindicated. They were friends again. Why, oh why, couldn't it have happened sooner? So much time had been wasted.

Jay had seemed so wantonly sexy; all wild-eyed and grinning. God, how she had missed the piquant potency of the sexual magnetism that existed between them. The attraction was still spiritual verging on the physical; she found the dark mind behind the eyes much more seductive than the body, but she had begun to want him so, so very badly.

As for the kiss, she was still reeling from the sheer force of it. She hadn't realised what had hit her until it was all over and she was walking away from him. It had felt as though she'd been hit very hard on the side of her face by something rubbery with bristles; her left cheek still stung where the stubble had grazed her skin. She wouldn't have been surprised to discover that he had drawn blood.

Kim's elation was succeeded by dread dejection. The following morning, a Saturday, she woke to find her mind shrouded in a cold, grey miasma of longing. She might never she Jay again after he went back to Manchester!

She went for a long walk through the fields behind her home to clarify her thoughts. What did she want? She had never asked herself that question before and doing so brought tears to her eyes. She knew the answer only too well; she wanted to see Jay again, just once before he went away. But how could she without running the risk of history repeating itself? She didn't want to bring that kind of hatred down on her again. That would be too much to bear.

Her conversation with Jay had left her all fired up; she had felt capable of doing anything, all her fears and uncertainties for the future had evaporated. If only she had been able to preserve that blessed state of mind she wouldn't need Jay any more. But no; one kiss couldn't sustain her forever. Talking to Jay had always been an elixir to Kim, with him and him alone was she truly able to be herself without any inhibitions. She could be bad with him and still feel good about it. At least, however, she knew that he didn't hate her and that somewhere he was being himself and doing his own thing; that was some comfort. But not enough. Was it really asking too much to be able to talk to him one more time before he disappeared again? Did she truly risk alienating him all over again if she tried to get in touch with him?

Kim closed her eyes briefly and took a deep breath. God! Wasn't this stupid! She was becoming paranoid about Jay's paranoia! It simply wasn't worth twisting herself into knots over him. She could almost feel her heart tearing itself in two.

For far too long now she had been afraid to want, for fear of denial and disappointment. Was that why she found it so hard to admit to herself what she felt for him? That and the fact that she knew he wouldn't want her to have feelings for him – he would view it as a millstone around his neck.

Kim had grown accustomed to rejection being her daily bread. Jay was so fortunate to have the band and his mates; what she wouldn't give to have what he had. Yet, didn't the fact that he got on so well with her imply they were alike in some way? Kim smiled ironically to herself. She bet that thought would send a shiver down his spine and make his skin crawl.

What the hell? *Carpe diem*! She would ring him on Monday.

*

Kim had had a driving lesson first thing on Monday morning. She was just about to open the garden gate after returning home when she happened to glance up the road to her left. In the distance she noticed a small blonde figure approaching. He looked vaguely familiar... no, it couldn't be, but yes it was... Jay. The man raised both arms in an arc above his head and waved at her. Kim hesitated for a moment then waved back and started to run towards him. She couldn't believe her luck! What an incredible coincidence, she was saved! Life could be wonderfully strange at times.

"Hi."

"Hello," he replied, half mumbling. His mouth looked a little strange.

"I thought I'd better wave in case you thought I thought you were psycho."

"Oh, thanks Jay. Actually you needn't have bothered, I didn't really recognise you for sure until you waved."

"Oh right. I wish I'd known," he said in a low voice.

"Look, would you like to go for a walk with me some time before you go away? I would rather that you didn't remember me as Hannibal Lector's little sister."

"Yeah, that would be, right... Umm, I don't know, I've just been to the dentist and my mouth still feels funny, so I'm not really up to talking."

Kim looked disappointed.

"Besides, I'm catching a train in a couple of hours and I have to pack."

The look of anxiety on Kim's face deepened. Finally he said, "Okay, so long as you do most of the talking."

Kim exhaled softly.

"Well, what do you want to talk about?" he asked.

"Tell me about your music. How do you write your songs?"

"I write them down whenever and wherever they come to me: when I'm on the bus, or eating, or anything."

"Oh... right," Kim's voice sounded distant.

"I don't like to get too emotional, otherwise it just turns into a pile of crap."

Kim was silent.

"Okay," he continued, "I've got a question for you. What are your theories on dreams?"

Kim smiled, "Actually, I had a really weird dream a couple of nights ago, which was probably inspired by you, although you weren't in it."

Jay shot her a piercing look.

"Indirectly, not directly; as I said, you weren't in it," she said quickly. "Okay, I'll give you my dream theory first. Umm, I think that when we dream we sometimes become aware of our true feelings and attitudes and how we might react under certain circumstances if there were no socially conditioned restraints on us. I think that the subconscious self has more integrity than the conscious self."

"Why?"

"Because the visceral and not the rational self is dominant in our dreams."

"So you believe in an absolute reality?"

"I sure do. When the quantum-mechanical wave function crashes, that's it, you have certainty."

"What wave function? I've never seen any wave function," Jay sneered in mock contempt.

"You're not supposed to, it's a mathematical model. It's through maths and maths alone, not psychology, that reality can be perceived correctly."

"When I dream, I always feel as though something is being hidden from me."

"Maybe it's a personal thing."

They reached Jay's sister's house and went inside.

"Would you like a cup of tea or something? I can't have one at the moment because of my mouth, but I could make one for you."

"No thanks, I'm fine."

"Okay, tell me about your dream."

"Oh God, I wish I hadn't mentioned that, it will sound so shallow. Um okay then, right, um I had a dream about John Power of 'Cast' fame. In my dream he lifted me up and kissed me hard on my lips. It seemed to go on forever, I had my legs wrapped around his waist and everything. It was wonderful, it really was; I didn't want it to end. I felt terribly sad when I woke up, I wanted him to be in the room with me so badly."

"I have dreams like that," said Jay, looking Kim straight in the eye.

She blinked, "When I dream about men, which is rare, it's always someone real but unobtainable. The rest of the time my dreams are full of imaginary people whose existences I make up."

"You dream about strangers?" Jay sounded surprised.

"Yep, take this dream I had last night for instance; I dreamt that I was a war artist in a country torn apart by civil war. I was sharing a room on the third floor of a large building with two other girls. We started talking about swimming pools; they said that they preferred the shallow end, but I said that I only swam in the deep end. Then we started to talk about Jaws."

"Really? I tend to have dreams in which I try to kick someone in. I mean, I'm really weedy in real life, but..."

"I thought you did karate?" interrupted Kim looking at Jay's bare arms. They didn't look weedy to her.

"Yeah, well... but in my dreams, if I see someone who I don't like, I just go for them."

"I rarely have violence in my dreams." Kim paused, remembering a dream in which she had attacked Jay of her own free will with a running shoe. "But the one time I did, I wasn't able to hit my victim as hard as I wanted to..."

"I know, that happens to me – it takes a fucking age to actually punch someone."

"Mmm, anyway I did have a deeper reason for mentioning the John Power dream. I've been thinking a lot about this guy I know. He seemed really special, but the feelings I experienced on waking from the 'Cast' dream were exactly the same as I've had for him. Which just goes to show how superficial I am."

"So?"

"So dreams can shed light on your desires and motivations."

"Assuming you interpret them correctly."

"Of course." Kim paused and then frowned. "So how's Mandy doing at Sheffield?" she asked tentatively. Still caught up in your shadow, Jay?

"Not too good," he said flatly.

"Oh." Kim's voice was sombre.

"How much have I told you?"

"Only that she was doing some art course," replied Kim in a neutral tone.

"Oh... I'll start from the beginning then. I took her down to Sheffield on the Saturday and came back on the Monday. Then on the Friday her mum died."

Kim felt cold, "Oh, how awful. Poor girl!"

"Yeah, it really hit her bad, she and her mother were very close. She came home for the funeral. Everyone thought she would stay, but she didn't, she went back to Sheffield."

"I knew a girl at Cambridge whose big sister died of spinal cancer, it almost crucified her."

"Mandy hasn't been the same since. She's really let herself go. I gave her a good bollocking about it three weeks ago, but, I don't know, it's this grieving thing I guess; I don't know how long it takes."

"Did she expect it, or was it a sudden thing?"

"Her mum had been ill all summer, but it was still a shock. She's lost interest in everything."

A flicker of pain crossed Kim's face. "It's strange how people handle things differently," she began, "I don't mean to criticise her, but when I went through my own period of hell I didn't dwell on it at all. I just focused on my work and kept going. It was an emotional expedient; the physical pain was bad enough, if I had let it hurt me emotionally it would have killed me – literally. I can talk about it now and recall every wretched detail and it doesn't hurt me one jot. Pain can make you very pragmatic about suffering. It's over now, it's dead wood. Do you want to hear the full story?"

"Go for it," he said in a low voice.

Kim smiled briefly. "Okay... Don't worry, I won't dissolve into tears or anything. I've become adept at screening out my emotions. I think it began at the end of my second year at Cambridge. I had a boyfriend called Simon, in the year above me, who I liked a lot, and I do mean a lot. When he graduated and moved to London to become an actuary I was really cut up. So I started my final year under a cloud. I mean, on one level it was really good, I got to specialise in pure maths and drop the dreaded statistics completely, but I really missed Simon... he was the guy. I had already lost a lot of weight in the long vac, I just felt so... null. I didn't want to eat; there didn't seem to be any point. I guess I was using hunger to mask the emotional emptiness, so I could pretend to myself that I didn't really miss him all that much, I was merely hungry. I'd lost more than two stone by the time I went back. I remember when my director of studies saw me for the first time, he literally stepped back in amazement; it would have been almost funny if it hadn't been so tragic.

"Anyway, things went from bad to worse; I buried myself in my work. It became all important to me. I suppose I was seeking refuge in it from the pain I felt at losing Simon."

Kim swallowed and took a deep breath, "I was eating less and less as time went on. I just couldn't be bothered to feed myself. I'd lost interest in everything except maths. At the end it was awful, I weighed about four and a half stone."

"How much do you weigh now?"

"About seven and a half, so I'd lost about half my body mass. It was horrible. I couldn't walk ten metres without my legs beginning to ache. I didn't get tired, just slower and slower; little old ladies would overtake me in the street. It used to take me about five minutes to climb the three flights of stairs to my room in college. I had to more or less literally heave myself up one leg at a time. I couldn't use the primitive lift because I didn't have sufficient strength in my arms to push or pull the rail thing to open it. It was sheer torture.

"By that time I must have been eating into my cardiac muscle; my heart and the palms of my hands hurt all the time. My limbs were so stiff and weak that I barely had the strength to stretch or to raise my arms high enough to brush my hair. By some miracle I did get my degree; it was that which made me stop and turn my situation around. It made me feel that perhaps I was worth something after all, that I did have a future and that I did deserve to live.

"After that I never looked back. I looked awful at the time though, like a living corpse. It's terrifying when your own body begins to waste away before your very eyes; when you know that you're dying, but don't have the strength to reverse the process; you're caught in a vicious circle. At the time my work was of paramount importance; I had to get my degree, that came first. I simply didn't have the energy to halt my physical deterioration, I'd gone too far down that particular road. Mad, I know, but true.

"In a strange way I think I was subconsciously punishing myself for being fortunate enough to get into Cambridge. I guess that ultimately it was just one big guilt trip. I hadn't done anything to deserve Cambridge, it was simply my genetic right. It didn't seem fair that I should have what others didn't."

"That's just stupid," Jay's face was set in a sardonic mask.

"I know, I know, that's just how it was... as I said, what I did to myself wasn't consciously motivated. I didn't intend it to happen, that would have been just too screwy."

"You can say that again," he said drily.

"I guess that in the end it does all boil down to guilt; like 'Okay Kim, you're having the time of your life, albeit with a cortisol-clogged consciousness, but you can't have it all your own way, you have to suffer like everyone else in the world. And boy, did I suffer. I must have been permanently stressed out, physically and emotionally.

"Anyway, that's all in the past. I'm a much stronger person now, I feel really good about my life. I hate to sound all Californian, but it was a good learning experience. I will never, ever make that kind of mistake again." Kim stopped speaking and smiled at Jay. A challenge.

"You might not live to tell the tale next time." Poor Jay, he didn't seem to know what to make of it.

"Exactly." Her smile widened into a grin.

She's laughing at me, he thought.

"Didn't it fuck your mind up though?"

Kim's grin collapsed. "Not really, no. I know that an experience like that is supposed to devastate your self-confidence etc., but no, my mind was focused on my work. You know me, if I'm doing maths I'm in seventh heaven. I was too detached from my physical self to let its pain affect me too deeply. I was living for mathematics, I didn't have the time to pay attention to anything else. I never cried or felt sorry for myself; I'm an archetypal tough cookie when it comes to things like that. There's not a single shred of self-pity in me, not one scrap. Self-pity in never justified. I think that everyone is responsible for their own hurt and the extent to which they let it affect their lives. Physical suffering is a different matter, of course. No, there was never any 'Oh why did this happen to me?' crap. I knew why it did, it was because I was so very, very stupid. No, I'm incapable of that sort of thing. Now self-irony, that's another matter."

Kim paused, smiling into thin air. Turning back to a cynical looking Jay she said, "So what are you doing with the band at the moment?"

Jay took a deep breath, "Oh we're moving around a lot, playing at different places. Just trying to get noticed, basically. Before, when we were doing it around here, we were only playing at it. Now we're serious. I mean, we're not likely to get a record deal around here. The trouble is we're too good."

"Oh yeah?" drawled Kim, sounding more sarcastic than she had intended.

"The music we play is the music of the future, people round here just can't appreciate it. I'm not saying we're going to be the next big thing or anything, but we do belong to tomorrow."

"So do you do all the writing?"

"Yes..."

Cool.

"...I used to be a purist, but I try to make it more accessible now."

"Will you play me some of your music?"

"No."

"Awww," she teased.

"I'm not going to sing to you."

"Can't you just tell me the lyrics?"

"No." He sounded adamant.

"Okay." She shrugged her shoulders.

"I'll tell you about an idea I'm working on, though. I was watching one of those Saturday morning kids' shows a few weeks ago; they were discussing unwanted pregnancies and what to do if one happened.

They mentioned adoption etc., but no one said anything about abortion – which I think is the only solution..."

"So do I," interrupted Kim. Jay looked at her sharply then continued with what he had been saying.

"It's like they were afraid it would be politically incorrect to mention it or something. So I wrote this song about a woman who's raped by a real bastard. She wants to get rid of it, but all she hears are the voices of her family and friends telling her to keep it. In the end she caves in to all the pressure and has it. Then, because it has the genes of the bastard rapist it grows up to rape and the cycle begins again... In the end it gets drunk and kills its mother. The last line is – 'But at least a life was saved.'"

"Irony."

"Not really. Most of the people who listen to music are stupid, so you have to give them a little something to figure out at the end to let them think that they're being clever."

"Huh! What contempt!" Did he realise how bitter he sounded?

Kim frowned as though about to say more, then relaxed and smiled.

"Remember I once told you that I have a friend, Chris, who's in a band?"

"Sort of."

"Well, they used to practice all day during the summer vac in the rhythm guitarist's parents' shed... real loud. They were going to soundproof it, but couldn't because it had an asbestos roof, or something like that. Anyway, someone complained to the council that they were a live band and were creating too much noise and this man turned up with a sound meter in order to get some concrete evidence. It was so funny, they just sat there watching him not playing a note. In the end Chris wrote a song about it with the two lines..." Kim took a deep breath and said in a low, rough voice:

"'He waited all night to get some proof,
But the door was only open 'cos of the asbestos roof.'"

Jay made a hollow laughing sound.

"I hope you don't mind me saying this, but I expect there's someone like me in the novel you've written."

"No. Why do you think that?" Huh! Such arrogance, you're so vain...'

"Because writers are supposed to draw inspiration from their own experiences."

"Maybe... But no, there's no one like you in it and I'll tell you why. I began writing it in October, that's when the ideas began to flood in. (I'd tried to write others before then but they got put on the back burner when I got the inspiration for the one I've just written.) It all came together in January, that's when I began to type it up. I finished the first draft in February, on February the fifteenth to be exact..."

"As if the date matters."

"Yeah, well," she laughed. "Anyway you were... purposefully avoiding me throughout that period, I couldn't have created a character based on you. It would have been too painful."

"Yeah." He sounded as if he understood.

Kim bit her lip and frowned. "Remember that day in August when you asked me to have sex with you? Why did you say 'but don't say yes or no'? I got the impression that you weren't sure about it."

"I needed to sort it out in my own mind first. I didn't know whether I wanted it or whether I just needed to get a shag out of my system... I don't care about messing women about, but I didn't want to fuck myself up."

Much to her own astonishment, Kim didn't flinch an inch. She wondered if long exposure to Jay had desensitised her finer feelings.

"Nice." She said flatly. Didn't she just love his casual brutality.

"So did you want it in the end?"

"Yes..."

Kim smiled slowly.

"...and I think you did too."

Her smile hit the deep freeze. She involuntarily fingered the collar of her shirt, suddenly feeling very hot.

"Then you went to pieces and I thought 'Fucking hell, what would it have been like if we'd had sex? Fatal attraction!'"

"I think not. That's too stereotypical."

Kim looked at Jay, taking in the strength in his neck and shoulders. He didn't look as sexy as he had on Friday, but he was still very, very desirable. For some stupid reason she still wanted him. Did he feel it too?

"So how often do you have sex with Mandy?" she asked with enormous casualness.

Jay seemed about to say something then stopped. "I wouldn't tell my best mate that, so I'm not going to tell you."

"But..."

"Okay," he said, "I'll tell you if you tell me why you want to know."

He was grinning. He felt it too.

"Umm... it's because I've never had sex with anyone and I want to know how these things work," she lied in a near monotone.

"You have," he said flatly, staring intently at her face.

"No I haven't," she replied in a tone of voice which left him with no choice but to believe her. Kim could be a good actress when she wanted.

"But you said..."

"I neither affirmed nor denied that I had. I simply let you believe what you wanted to."

"You fucking liar." Not the most appropriate choice of adjective.

Kim laughed. He looked absolutely thunderstruck. It was so funny, he actually believed in her false claim to innocence.

"So you're a virgin?" He was beginning to feel the heat again.

"Well that would follow, wouldn't it?" Boy, was he quick.

"Do you have any sexual feelings?" He continued to stare fixedly at her.

"Mmm," she nodded, staring back with equal intensity. Like right now. Did he want her again now that he thought she was pure? Did he want to be the one? Would the eroticism of innocence make her a star fuck in his eyes?

"Do you masturbate?"

Yuk! She thought they'd been through that before. Kim looked away from him. "No," she said, her eyes dull. Let him think her untouched by all, including herself.

"Why not?"

"Because I have no desire to," she replied flatly. Too late. She had pulled back from the edge.

Jay blinked, suddenly aware that he had been staring at her as though transfixed. "Actually I haven't had a shag since... well, I'm not going to tell you that." He frowned then looked at his watch. "I'll have to throw you out now, I've got some packing to do."

Oh Jay, don't you want to see how brave I am?

"That's okay," she murmured. He was scared. She had challenged him and he was scared; afraid that he might not be up to it. What a wimp!

He walked with her to the door.

"Good luck, Jay."

"Take care, and good luck with whatever you're doing."

"Teaching."

"Oh that's easy."

"Not if the kids gang up on you."

Kim felt an insidious sense of anti-climax creep over her.

"If I hadn't made last Friday happen, would you ever have wanted to speak to me again?" she asked.

"I might have said 'hi' if I saw you, but that's all."

Kim felt numb.

"You didn't really believe that I was trying to terrorise you?"

"I did at the time, but it all seems so daft now."

"Good."

★

The following Friday evening found Jay's dad, Stewart, sitting in his lounge going through some case notes. The room was filled with soft evening sunlight and the sombre sound of Samuel Barber's *Adagio for Strings*. All was peaceful. His wife was outside, working in the garden; something urgent concerning the pansies.

Suddenly a spasm of pain gripped his temples. Raising his head from the notes, he put a hand to his forehead and closed his eyes. He could sense that a headache was about to develop. Without warning, his body rocked forward involuntarily as a terrific pain exploded behind his eyes. He felt as though he had been hit on the back of his head with a cricket bat.

The pain continued to pulse for a few seconds then subsided into nothing. Stewart blinked and shook his head. Returning his attention to his notes he started to read... that was strange, the words didn't seem to make sense; he recognised them yet they had no meaning for him. He closed his eyes again, then opened them only to discover that his field of vision had been halved. Perhaps he had better lie down. Thwack! Another bolt of pain seared through his mind, consciousness receded and he slid into oblivion.

Chapter Eleven

Soliloquy

Staring up at the glowering sky, Kim sensed the sharp threat of a thunderstorm in the air. I'll run through the cemetery, she thought as she pulled on her running shoes, her mind lost in gothic musing. The ambience would be incredible.

The cemetery was empty when she got there. Kim was glad of this; everything was cool and green, and it was simply delicious to be able to savour the calm, sombre atmosphere all alone. Besides, she hated to be seen when she was running in a place like this; the presence of other humans drew her attention to the thump and crunch of her feet on the ground and made her feel that she was violating a sacred silence.

On jogging slowly past the fresh graves, Kim was reminded of broken pieces of wedding cake strewn with a pastel confetti of wreaths and bouquets. In the more ancient parts of the cemetery the pathway was covered with a soft, green moss and bordered with tall trees covered in apple-green, heart-shaped leaves. The headstones were scattered about in the long grass like discarded chess pieces, tilting amongst clumps of bluebells, buttercups and briar.

Kim stood still for some time staring up at the marble statue of a woman, overshadowed by a lush, dark green yew tree and letting her hot skin drink in the cool air. The figure wore a long, loose robe; it was so skilfully sculptured that it almost seemed to ripple in the breeze. The inscription at its base read 'Blessed are the pure in heart for they shall see God'. What an exquisite sentiment. For a fleeting moment Kim almost wished that she believed.

Walking on, a white object lying in the grass caught Kim's eye. She bent down and picked it up. It was a beautiful carving of an angel's hand. Kim decided to take it with her. No one would miss it.

She retraced her steps to the newer plots. On emerging from a group of sturdy oak trees, Kim was startled to find Jay bending over a recently filled and beflowered grave. She reeled... "His dad! Oh God, if he sees me now, he'll feel that I'm intruding on his grief... he'll never forgive me!"

Kim broke free from her state of temporary petrification and tried to move silently away. As she did, Jay turned his head and recognised her. For one absurd moment she had a vision of herself laying the angel's hand down by the grave in silent sympathy for Jay's sorrow. Jay shuddered, his face reddening. Kim felt a silent scream begin to form deep inside her head. 'It's happening again,' her mind cried, 'I can't bear it. It will tear my heart out!' Without thinking, she raised the stone hand and struck Jay on the back of his head.

The blow crushed his skull, and he toppled. His head hit the headstone of his father's grave with a sickening thud and he lay still. Kim stared in horror at Jay's inert and bloodied body. Blood raged in her temples, making her feel as though her head would burst. A wave of nausea washed through her and she swayed, feeling faint. Get a grip, girl! Swallowing, she raised her hand to her brow and looked about her. She was alone.

Kim grabbed the hand from where she had let it fall after hitting Jay, and fled. She sped through the trees, jumping over the graves and bramble bushes. On reaching the boundary fence she climbed through it into the fields beyond. Once more she took off like a gazelle and ran and ran, along hedgerows and furrows, in a desperate, adrenalin-fuelled flight. No one saw her.

Eventually she stopped, her body seized by a crippling stitch and her chest heaving. Blood continued to thud through the pulsating veins and arteries in her legs. She felt sick and dizzy and very, very hot, as if she had run into a net of heat and been enveloped by it. Gradually her breathing slowed as the erratic expansions and contractions of her ribcage became more rhythmic. She felt sweat begin to trickle down her spine. Examining the piece of stone in her hand, she saw that there was blood on it: his blood. Kim began to shudder uncontrollably and was forced to bend over and put her free hand on one knee until the trembling had ceased. She was thankful that she hadn't eaten anything before going on her run. Removing a handkerchief from around her neck, she used it to wipe the blood from the fragment of sculpture, then retied it about her throat; her heart continued to beat savagely in her chest as she did this.

A strong wind had begun to blow. Looking up at the sky Kim could see heavy clouds rolling in, full of rain. Now to get rid of the offending weapon. Kim retraced some of her steps and headed for the bridge high above the abandoned railway line. Once there, she flung the hand onto the metal tracks below. It broke up on impact with the steel. Kim ran down and scattered the fragments into the dust and debris between the rails with her feet.

The air felt much cooler now. She knew that rainfall was imminent. The clouds kept pace with her as she jogged homeward and a soft drizzle began to fall, so fine that she was hardly aware of its touch on her skin. Kim's mind and body felt numb and the condensing moisture seemed to form a cocoon around her, separating her from the rest of the world, and just for the moment, while she was running and the adrenalin was still in her bloodstream, from the... thing she had done. It would hit home hard enough when she got back to the house. Reality could wait until then.

*

On returning home, Kim went straight to the bathroom. Looking in the mirror, she untied the handkerchief knotted around her neck. There were traces of dried blood on her throat. She moistened a finger, rubbed the dark red flecks from her skin, put the finger back in her mouth and tasted Jay's blood.

Sensing that the last traces of adrenalin were draining from her blood, Kim seized the sweat-sticky clumps of hair which clung to her scalp and pulled them away from her face. Then, returning her attention to the mirror, she considered her reflection: a young, oval-shaped face, sprinkled with a cinnamon dusting of freckles and enclosing large, brown eyes; the essence of innocence and honesty, framed with ridiculously red hair. She was a good girl. Not a killer. No way! And yet, if Jay was dead, and somehow she knew he was, she was exactly that; a murderer, trapped in the body of an *ingénue*. If would be horribly funny, if it wasn't so horribly real.

Looking out of the window, Kim saw that the storm had broken. She went into her bedroom, lay down on the pale-blue carpet and watched the downpour. Was he dead? Was the rain washing his blood into the ground? Kim felt numb. Why was this? She had probably killed him, and yet nothing, no adrenalin-accelerated heartbeat... just... nothing. Except this maddening state of benumbed calm.

Why?

Oxygen starvation?

Exhaustion?

She had left Jay unconscious. Was he still there? Was he dead or dying? Well, she had done it now, hadn't she? Just when she'd begun to get her life back together again! Was it fate or just bad genes? There was no way of getting away from it, she had started something which she wouldn't be able to stop.

Kim felt drained. Her entire body ached, yet sleep eluded her. Why, when her mind was spinning with words and images, did she feel nothing? She knew exactly what she had done, it was all too clear in her head; she could picture every detail in her mind's eye... his body lying there... yet nothing. It was too unreal, too terribly stark and clinical to be absorbed and accepted by her psyche. Oh God, it was awful.

She rolled away from the window. As she did so, her eye caught a flash of light reflected from a tiny shard of glass lying on the carpet. She picked it up, put it into her mouth and swallowed.

★

Jay was dead. Kim had read the report in the local evening paper, then removed the picture of the Jay look-alike from her bedroom wall, torn it to shreds and defenestrated the pieces.

One blow, just one blow, and the unhappy presence of the headstone... But then, she had hit him hard... maybe he'd had an unusually soft skull. Oh God, she had killed him, she had actually... killed him. Strange words! Kim found it hard to form them in her mind. She tried to say them out loud. For some weird reason she could do that easily, as though reciting the words of a poem or a play... *fiction, mere fiction.*

Oh God, what had she done?

What had made her capable of such violence?

Had she felt more for him than she'd allowed herself to admit? If so, why hadn't she been able to keep control of her emotions, instead of giving them full rein at that one fatal instant in which she had struck him? Her action hadn't been premeditated, of that she was certain. She hadn't been aware of feeling any enmity towards him; he had been little more than a distraction to her. Yet he had rejected her, and it had hurt that someone whose existence she valued should want to slight her... and that very same hurt had proved itself to be the latent poison which had made her capable of killing him.

That was it, self! She had acted in self-defence, to protect herself from further emotional damage. She had wanted to rid herself of the source of continuing pain that was Jay. Everything was chillingly clear.

How could she have been so selfish? He had been mourning his father and she had first trespassed on his grief and then struck him down and left him to die. She had thought only of herself and her own pain; she had been too wrapped up in her egocentric little world to see things as they really were.

The truth seared through her self-indulgent half-truths and exaggerations. She could almost feel the toxic sweat of her twisted delusions beginning to eat into her flesh. She was going to have to play a very high price for playing the voyeur of her own emotions and viewing her life as if it were a fragment of fiction. She had possessed no real feeling for him. She had just been playing silly games, trying to live out a fantasy of her own devising. Jay had been nothing to her; the pain he had caused her had been intense but superficial. She should have ignored it not wallowed in it, giving it an artificial life simply so that she could use it as an inspirational focus for the so-called tragedies of her past.

Kim felt appalled by her stupidity and self-obsession. Jay had taken her on an ego-trip. That was why she had liked him so much; he had made her feel interesting and original... alive. She hadn't felt anything for him, her emotions had been mere parodies of the real thing.

But what frightened Kim most was how quick and easy it had been to kill him. She hadn't had time to stop and think about what she was doing. She had become so mesmerised by her sense of injury that she had simply dealt the death blow with as much force as she could muster, then fled, like the pathetic little coward she was. It was so horribly insane... something which happened to other people, not to her.

*

The first few days following Jay's murder were pure torture for Kim. She felt shaken to the core, as though she had been physically beaten up. Kim knew what hell was, she had been there and back during her attempt at self-starvation, but that was mere candyfloss compared to what she was now experiencing. Self-hatred loomed over her, like a dark cloud on the horizon of her consciousness. She tried to cry, but found that she couldn't; tears seemed so superfluous, as did the dry heavings of her thorax. Every fibre of her being craved release from this torment, but there was no relief in sight. She was back in the murkworld again.

At night, in bed, the darkness seemed to be thick with her guilt, and again, Jay's death was the first thing to enter her mind when she woke up in the morning. The pathways of her mind seemed to be paved with razor-sharp shards of glass; there was nothing she thought of which didn't lead back to Jay via one tortuous route or another. She was still able to sleep; she had always been able to do that, but the waking oppression was crushing her. She felt as though she would suffocate.

Everything in her world seemed hollow, it was as if her entire existence had imploded into the singularity of Jay's murder. Kim's life had been swept away and replaced by a vacuum. Jay was dragging her soul into the grave with him. No matter what she did or where she went, his image would rise up before her mind, eager to draw blood. She had never tasted such bitter torment.

It was as if Jay's death defined her very being, as though, if someone cut her, she would bleed his blood. It had become a cancer eating away at her sanity.

Walking in the early morning isolation of the park, Kim faced the all too real possibility of the end of her physical freedom. Yes, that was the dread thought she must avoid at all cost. She had stopped looking at the evening paper, but the fear was always there, like a snake coiled round her neck, whispering terrible words in her ear. Perhaps she ought to kill herself now, to get it over and done with. Wasn't that what she deserved?

Kim closed her eyes and swallowed. She had to stop this otherwise it would destroy her, in which case she might as well get down onto her hands and knees right now and grind her skull into the concrete. No, she wasn't going to let that happen; she had to confront her despair and quash it. One of the lessons she had learnt from previous bad times was that she mustn't dwell on the blackness, or propagate the pain. She wasn't going to make that mistake again. No way! She had to concentrate on driving out these feelings of desolation and guilt, and marshalling her inner calmness. Jay might be dead, but she couldn't bring him back by destroying herself. She wasn't going to twist in the wind for him unless she had to. What was done was done; it was irrevocable and therefore rendered all regrets meaningless, hopeless and obsolete. Dust to dust, ashes to ashes. She would be strong, she would not betray herself. No, she would survive it... but it was going to be hard, so very hard.

Yet something inside Kim held on, and would not let her be dragged down. No, she wasn't going to kill herself, not for him. Let the stark knowledge of what she had done haunt her forever, but there was no way she was going to destroy all she had achieved because of one... mistake. That wasn't as much of a euphemism as it might seem, for her act *had* been a mistake; no matter how heinous a crime or terrible the consequences, it was still a mistake. Her mistake.

She had had no intention to kill him, she had acted instinctively to protect herself from hurt to come. She had violated no natural law. Perhaps it was ultimately Jay's fault. Without those months of unrelenting hostility the whole sorry scenario might never have arisen. She would never have begun to dread his hatred. Yes, poor Jay, poor dead Jay, but poor Kim too. At least his suffering had been brief. Hers hadn't. And yes, he had caused her to suffer agony and he had known what he was doing. She hadn't, not in that fatal moment when she had hit out at him.

Something melted within Kim and as the ice began to retreat, so she began to relax and feel her vitality come back into bloom. She was still herself. Nothing could ever change that. Whatever happened, she would hold on to her identity. She had to, there was no other choice if she wanted to survive. She knew she had heroine potential, all she had to do was to tap into it. Besides, maybe there was hope, perhaps worldly retribution wasn't inevitable. Was it such an impossible dream?

She had to keep a grip on herself. She had struggled through too much hardship to falter now. She wasn't going to nullify her life for Jay. She must banish his ghost and focus on the future.

★

Time passed and still there was no knock at the door. One evening a report in the local paper claimed that twenty ecstasy tablets had been found on Jay's corpse and that a search of the flat which he shared with the rest of the band in Manchester had revealed a quantity of crack-cocaine and baking soda. The police were said to be considering the possibility that Jay's murder might be drugs related.

Chapter Twelve

Return of the Space Cowgirl

As time passed, Jay's death seemed to be less and less real to Kim.

It was as if, in spite of everything, she was gradually disassociating herself from the crime and from her guilt.

Three months after his death she paid a dawn visit to his grave.

Standing in front of the headstone in the half-light of early morning, Kim found it hard to take in the fact that Jay was directly beneath her and that they were in such proximity. It seemed stranger still that all that remained of him was a corpse in a casket, stewing in its own liquor.

If only she had a lock of his hair, something to remind her that they had once been friends. But she had nothing except the handkerchief stained with his blood, now sewn into the heart of her battered childhood teddy bear. Still, the past was immutable; nothing could erase the time she had spent with him or the words they had said to each other.

Killing Jay had blown her life apart, severing her from her immediate past. She was now a murderer, a pariah through circumstance not choice. Would she ever be able to distance herself from her dread deed? His shade still haunted her.

There was hope. She would be moving on in the coming September, away from the shadows of her past.

There was no way she was going to live her life with her heart shot through with fear. She would surf, not sink; through life, through pain, through everything. It was Jay who was a blank on the face of the living world. Not her. Putting her hand into the back pocket of her jeans, Kim pulled out a piece of paper.

Dear Jay,

I apologise for writing, but I've got so much poetry (for want of a better word) in me at the moment, that I just had to, even though I don't know whether or not you'll get this letter.

I guess I'm going through a kind of spiritual renaissance: post-emotional burn out. (The days of doing dangerous and unnecessary things to myself are long gone.) Funny how the flames seem to burn more brightly the second time around.

Chris has lent me his acoustic guitar on condition that I pay for any strings I break – there's confidence for you! I've kind of developed a yen to make my own music, although for the moment I'm keeping very quiet about the new sounds I'm making. I'm hoping he'll let me play his electric guitar too, however I'm not very optimistic on that score. He still hasn't forgiven me for knocking it over when I walked into his room without realising that the sacred instrument was leaning against the other side of the door.

Furthermore, I think my flute has developed supernatural powers, weird things happen whenever I play it: clocks stop and books fall over. Honestly, it's true! Probably due to some kind of resonance, I guess. All the same, it's pretty unnerving.

I hope you don't see this letter as an attempt to terrorise you.

(I'm sorry I had to say that, I guess I'm still a little edgy that way.)

It's just that I'm a little impatient to be heard by another human being.

I don't expect you to write back. You have the luxury of callousness, lucky/unlucky you, but if you do reply it'll be cool. I don't feel as though I'm sending my words out into a void. I figure you'll catch my drift, we've always been on the same wavelength, just maybe a little out of phase at times. I like you so much; you're an original thinker. There's so much I'd like to ask you about music and stuff, but maybe for now I'm just glad that if ever we met on the astral plane you wouldn't kick dust in my eyes. Or would you?

Hope you read me, buddy,
love
Kim.

Kim kissed the letter once, then crumpled it into an untidy ball and used it to wipe the tear stains from her cheeks. Raising her head, she smiled at the dawn cloudscape beneath the retreating stars, then walked away.